I0703042

Honeymoon for Seven

CHRIS KENISTON

Indie House Publishing

This book is a work of fiction. Names, characters, places and incidents are the product of the author's imagination or are used fictionally. Any resemblance to actual events, locales, or persons, living or dead, is coincidental.

Copyright 2024 Christine Baena
Print Edition

All rights reserved. No part of this book may be used for the training of or use by artificial intelligence, nor reproduced, scanned, redistributed or transmitted in any form or by any means, print, electronic, mechanical, photocopying, recording, or otherwise, without prior written permission of Author.

Indie House Publishing

MORE BOOKS
By Chris Keniston

The Billionaire Barons of Texas
Just One Date
Just One Spark
Just One Dance
Just One Take
Just One Taste
Just One Shot
Just One Chance
Just One Mistake
Just One Family
Just One Rodeo
Just One Surprise
Just One Look

Hart Land
Heather
Lily
Violet
Iris
Hyacinth
Rose
Calytrix
Zinnia
Poppy
Picture Perfect

Farraday Country
Adam
Brooks
Connor
Declan
Ethan

Finn
Grace
Hannah
Ian
Jamison
Keeping Eileen
Loving Chloe
Morgan
Neil
Owen
Paxton
Quinn

Honeymoon Series
Honeymoon for One
Honeymoon for Three
Honeymoon for Four
Honeymoon for Five
Honeymoon for Six
Honeymoon for Seven

Aloha Romance Series:
Aloha Texas
Almost Paradise
Mai Tai Marriage
Dive Into You
Look of Love
Love by Design
Love Walks In
Shell Game
Flirting with Paradise

Surf's Up Flirts:
(Aloha Series Companions)
Shall We Dance
Love on Tap
Head Over Heels
Perfect Match
Just One Kiss
It Had to Be You
Cat's Meow

ACKNOWLEDGMENT

To Cheryl Lucas for saving the day—again!

CHAPTER ONE

"How many people does it take to pack one suitcase?" Ginnie Ummarino had been trying to pack for her cruise for most of the week, and every time she opened the new wheeled luggage, someone would stick their two cents in.

"Four," several voices chorused, punctuated with giggles.

Heaven knew that Ginnie loved her sisters Mina and Jo, and her mother Antoinette with all her heart, but every once in a while, it was nice to be able to make up her own mind without a group discussion. Or in this case, pack a suitcase without Jo adding spiked heels, Mina taking out the granny bathrobe, and her mother slipping in every over-the-counter medication known to man. Anyone looking in her bag would think that a lady of the evening was invading the Amazon jungle. The only med missing was snake bite antidote, because her mother had cramps, nausea, migraines, diarrhea, cuts and bruises covered.

"You have to take these." Jo held out the strand of pearls that Ginnie had bought on their first cruise together. She'd only been on two cruises in her life and both her sisters had been with her each time. Going solo felt…well…weird.

But she did agree about the pearls. "These will be perfect for formal night." That was the reason she'd bought them in the first place. That and a treat for her practical self. All her life she'd been described as the practical one of the Ummarino sisters. While she didn't mind it, mostly because she *was* practical, she didn't love it either. Her one and only true recent rebellion had been buying impractical pearls.

Though it could be argued since they fit in anywhere under any circumstances, the splurge was still, well, practical.

"Now remember," Jo sat down on the bed by the suitcase, "talk to everyone. Don't stay in your room."

"And remember to smile." Mina sat on the other side of the suitcase. "Don't get lost in your own thoughts, which causes you to frown."

"I do not." Hands tucking her favorite shorts into the corner of the suitcase, her head snapped up to glare at her sister. "I smile all the time."

"True." Standing with her hands in the closet, her mother bobbed her head. "A beautiful smile that would win over any good man, but you do get lost in your own thoughts."

And there her mother went with a good man routine again. Leaving on the cruise was going to be easy. Enjoying herself wouldn't be a chore, after all, even on her own. A nice relaxing cruise would be a wonderful vacation, but coming home alone, that was going to be difficult. Her mother seemed to have come to the conclusion that all it would take to marry off her stubbornly single daughters was a cruise. Especially since each one of her sisters had come home with a fiancé after exactly that. Her mom was going to be horribly disappointed when Ginnie returned as single as the day she was born.

"Which of these two dresses are you taking?" Her mother held up the two new cocktail dresses she'd bought for the formal night. One had been a classic black which fell to just below her knees with a little beadwork on the short sleeves and a respectable scoop neckline. Her dark hair and eyes always showed well in black. The other had been a bit of a splurge. Deep purple, with gold accent threading, this dress was just a tad above her knees and showed a drop more cleavage. Mina and the saleswoman had insisted she couldn't leave the store without it. Truth was, she loved how it made her figure look, showing off just enough curve without emphasizing—as her mother referred to them—her childbearing broad hips.

"A little color is good for you." To Ginnie's surprise,

her mother handed her the purple dress.

"I'll take them both." Ginnie was not going to leave home without having a backup safe dress in case she chickened out. No matter what her mother thought, she wasn't on this cruise to find a husband. Her entire section at work had been rewarded for their last project with a cruise vacation. She'd come within an inch of giving it to one of her sisters to take their husband on a second honeymoon, not that either of them needed it. Anytime the couples were together, they still looked at each other like they could eat the other with a spoon. Some days it made her smile to see her sisters so darn happy, some days when they were all lovey-dovey it made her want to gag. But she'd take lovey-dovey over unhappy any day of the week.

"I still think you should have talked your cousin Giovanni into going with you." Her mama put the two dresses neatly beside the suitcase. "Maybe you could have helped him find a nice girl. Make him and Uncle Tony happy."

All three sisters rolled their eyes but said nothing. For years, Uncle Tony couldn't understand that her cousin Giovanni was actually very happy with his bachelor lifestyle. The guy was friendly, handsome, and had a smile that had women falling at his feet. What more could a bachelor ask for? She and her sisters figured the guy was going to be like Warren Beatty or George Clooney; with no biological clock, he'd just enjoy life until he was too old to keep up, then he'd marry and have a slew of kids. Though George only had two—but still.

Gently folding the two cocktail dresses across the top of the suitcase, she lowered the lid and zipped it shut. "And done." Her stomach turned with a little bit of nervous anticipation. This would be her first time vacationing alone. Well, alone if you ignored the five thousand other people on the ship. She enjoyed the trivia and other evening shows, and was more than ready to relax on a deck chair with a favorite book and soak up some vitamin sea. She'd be okay, would have lots of fun. Now, she only needed to repeat that to herself a few hundred more times and all would be well.

"Great toast." Nick Maroney slapped his dad on the back. The toast was not too long, not too short, and heartfelt.

"I didn't get a chance to do it when Theresa and Chuck married in Vegas." His father looked momentarily sullen. When Chuck died in a car accident just over two years ago, Nick's sister was devastated. They'd been such a happy couple. The day little Phoebe was born was bittersweet. Such a joy to have a new life and such sadness that her father wasn't here to see her. The light in his father's eyes flickered bright again. "She's happy again."

Nick couldn't argue. His sister had been working with Alan at the same elementary school for a few years. He'd lost his wife a little over a year before Chuck had died. What had started out as friendship and support, eventually bloomed into romance, and now, here they all were preparing for their own version of the *Brady Bunch* sans one.

"What I still don't understand is why would anyone in their right mind want to go on a honeymoon with their children." That had baffled Nick ever since his sister and Alan announced they'd decided on a honeymoon cruise and were taking all their kids with them.

"Not many people have to worry about children on a honeymoon." His father's grin stretched across his face.

"No." Nick chuckled. "And certainly not a honeymoon for seven."

"It will be fun. Your mother and I needed a good excuse for a nice vacation."

Somehow, Nick doubted that corralling five children, two of whom barely knew their new grandparents, was going to be much of a vacation for his parents, but it would at least allow the honeymooners some time to, well, honeymoon.

"Don't they look so happy?" Nick's mom Rose sidled up to her husband. "Nothing beats seeing your grown children happy."

Uh-oh. If he didn't make an exit and quickly, he knew what his mother's next words were going to be. Like a good Italian mother, Rose D'Angelo Maroney didn't believe her son could possibly be happy until he was married with children, preferably a lot of them. "I see Theresa. I think she's calling me over. See you two later."

Holding his fist to his mouth, his dad coughed just a bit, thankfully distracting his mother. "Excuse me."

"That cough is getting worse."

His father shrugged. "Dumb allergy season. At least I didn't cough through the speech."

"Still." His mother frowned. "I'll make you a honey lemon toddy when we get home. Can't have you coming down with anything before Thursday when the ship sails."

"No worries, Rose, dear. With all the excitement, I forgot to take my allergy pill today."

Rose kissed her husband's cheek and smiled. "You did good, handsome."

His father beamed. Whether fighting or flirting, his parents were always passionate. He couldn't fathom loving someone so much after so many years. He'd known a few women in his life who he'd thought could be the one, and yet, as time passed, so did the elusive devotion he knew he'd need to have what his parents had. Though he wouldn't mind having it with a little less volatility.

"Mrs. Maroney." The wedding coordinator came up beside his mom. "Your daughter is getting ready to toss her bouquet."

"The night is going by so quickly." His mother nodded at the woman, linked arms with her husband at one side and her son at the other. "Let's go."

Theresa stood ready to toss the bouquet. When she spotted her mother, she smiled and turning, waved the thing over head before letting it rip through the small hall. Nick had no idea why this old ritual was such a big deal, but every single woman in the place gathered in the middle of the dance floor and when the bouquet flew across the room, anyone would have thought his sister was giving away gold.

By the time the reception was over, Nick was beyond

exhausted. Partying all night was not in his playbook anymore. As soon as Theresa and Alan drove off into the night, Nick kissed his mom and dad and headed home, collapsing on his bed without bothering to strip out of his tuxedo, though he did take a few minutes to shuck the jacket and undo the bow tie.

When his phone rang the next morning, he wished he'd turned the darn thing off. "Hello."

"Nicky, we have a problem." His mother sounded distressed.

Flinging the blankets to one side, he sat up. "What's wrong, Mom?"

"Your father is testing positive for Covid."

"Did you take him to the hospital?"

"No. His oxygenation is high, his fever is low, but his cough in lingering. The doctor sent him something to take. Says he's going to feel better soon."

"Oh, good. So what's the problem?"

"The doctor says he won't test negative in time for the cruise. You're going to have to take your father's place."

CHAPTER TWO

Unpacked, Ginnie had hung up her dresses, put away her shoes, and folded clothes in the drawers. Every few minutes, she glanced out the window at the shipping channel. In a few hours the view would be totally different—she'd be basking in rolling seas, blue skies, and salty breezes.

This whole trip alone felt strange. Mina couldn't join her because she and her husband were hosting an anniversary celebration for his parents. No way she could back out of that. Jo had done everything she could to juggle her schedule but in the end, the schedule won. Since none of her friends were available for that much time either, and Ginnie was too practical to let a free trip go to waste, here she was sailing alone.

Changed into her favorite yellow sundress, it was time to venture out of her cabin. She could do this. Meandering her way onto the upper deck, she leaned against the rail as a band played Calypso music, waiters passed by with trays of drinks, and the ship began to move. Excitement tickled her senses. She really did love cruising.

Her phone dinged, the sound startling her. Glancing down, it was from Jo. *Wish I was there.* Quickly she responded, *Me too!* Another few minutes and another ding. This time it was Mina. *Have a good time!* That was certainly the plan. After all, who takes a cruise to have a bad time? A waiter walked by and she took a yellow and red frozen drink. "What is this?"

"Marvelous Mango." The man smiled up at her.

"Sounds good." She waved the room card hanging around her neck and he used a handheld machine to record her purchase. So far, so good. Already she could feel the stress of everyday life rolling away.

Another ding. Now what? She'd run out of sisters.

You okay? Of course. Her mother.

Yes, Mama. Weather is wonderful. Not wanting to start a long conversation, she quickly typed. *Time to turn the phone off. See you when I get home.*

The breeze blowing in her hair, she sucked in a deep breath. Another layer of stress slid away. This was going to be a great trip. Exactly what she needed even if she hadn't realized it at the time she decided to come solo rather than give the cabin away. Now that the ship was on its way, all the shops on the promenade would be open. Time to check out the wares. Last cruise she picked up some nice bargains.

The other nice thing about being on a ship was that she could walk around with a drink and it didn't matter. Especially since she was a notoriously slow sipper and could nurse a drink for hours. The first day on the ship always felt like the most crowded. Everyone had the same idea to wander about and get their bearings. This cruise was no different—as a matter of fact, the promenade deck felt especially crowded with people mulling about and stopping in the middle of the walkway without warning, older folks scooting about in electric chairs, and kids running loose as if the ship was their private playground.

Stopping at the jewelry store window, she stared at the brightly lit display. Miscellaneous pieces caught her eye. She had no idea if the green stones were emeralds or glass, same with the dark blues and reds, but some were awfully pretty. Most of the people looking at the displays were smiling or laughing. A few folks tried on some pieces, others joked about their budgets and in their dreams. One poor man caught her eye. He'd been staring at a diamond ring. His expression a blank slate but his eye seemed oddly sad for a person who should be enjoying themselves on a fun-filled cruise.

Dragging her gaze away from the sad man and resisting the temptation to go inside and try a few rings on, she turned toward the next store and felt a weight slam into her legs.

Great. Just what she didn't need this trip, wayward children bouncing off passengers. When the weight remained and no apologies followed, she glanced behind her and then down. "Well, hello."

A little one, barely taller than Ginnie's knees, with long curls that hung over her shoulders and big blue eyes stared up at her. "Mommy."

Mommy. Quickly Ginnie glanced around her, looking for a frantic parent. Nothing. "Hello."

The cherub smiled. "Mommy."

Okay, looking at the kid's coloring, Ginnie doubted seriously that Mommy bore any resemblance to her Mediterranean genetics, but crouching to the little girl's level, she smiled back. "I guess we need to find your mommy."

Still grinning brightly, the little girl repeated "Mommy" even though she now had a clear view of Ginnie's face.

"No sweetie, but we'll find her."

"Mommy." The little girl flung her arms around Ginnie's neck and almost knocked her off her feet.

For the next few seconds, Ginnie scanned the people walking past and debated if she should risk the kid screaming her lungs off and just pick the child up and take her to the concierge, or if waiting here for her mom and dad to find her would be better.

The little girl continued to squeeze Ginnie's neck, and reflexively she hugged the child back. Shaking her head, she figured if the kid thought she was Mommy and didn't mind being hugged, standing up with her wouldn't be a problem. Obviously, the real Mommy wasn't looking for her so Ginnie would have to go find the woman.

"There you are," the rich deep voice floated over her like a warm shower.

Tipping her head back, her gaze locked with eyes the same beautiful shade of blue as the child still clinging to her neck.

The man hunched down beside them and looked straight into the little girl's eyes, smiling at her with the same wide grin. The resemblance was uncanny. "Your mommy is going to be very happy that I found you."

That silky smooth voice was slowly turning Ginnie's legs to mush. Why oh why were all the good men taken?

For just a few seconds, Nick thought his sister had found Phoebe. Once he got close enough to see the woman, he realized that little Phoebe had latched onto someone wearing a similar dress. He supposed when you're two years old, and standing up only seeing people's knees, one yellow dress and woman's legs must look like any other yellow dress and woman's legs.

"Oh, good. You found her." His sister Theresa came rushing up beside them. "I swear she's getting faster every day."

Even though her mother had arrived, Phoebe was still clinging to the stranger's neck and didn't show any sign of intending to let go.

The stranger must have concluded the same thing as she wrapped her arms around his niece and pushed to her feet. "I think she found me is more accurate."

"Come to Mommy, baby."

Phoebe frowned at her mother, then looked to the stranger and back. It took the child a few moments to decide that the stranger was not her mom and finally leaned toward his sister.

"That's my sweet girl." Theresa turned to face the other woman in yellow. "Thank you for keeping an eye on her. I'm a little overwhelmed with all these people and corralling five children."

The way the stranger's eyes rounded momentarily, she reflected the way he felt when he thought about going from three to five kids in the time it took to say *I do*.

"Oh, good. You found her." His mother, with a child in each hand, came rushing up to them, just slightly out of breath. "How can someone with such short legs move so fast?"

The stranger looked from one adult to the other then down to the two little kids. Her rather stoic expression shifted and she smiled at the two boys who looked nothing like either parent, and wiggling her fingers, waved at them. Immediately both boys smiled and waved back.

"I'm sorry. I should introduce myself. I'm Theresa Reidy, these are my daughters, Rachel and Monica."

Monica held out her favorite stuffed rabbit. "This is Bunny."

"Very nice to meet you, Bunny." The woman in yellow squatted to Monica's height, coaxing a wide smile from his younger niece.

"And this little munchkin," Theresa jostled the toddler on her hip, "is my daughter Phoebe."

The poor kid still studied the stranger with an intensity he'd never noticed before. Of course, he didn't really spend that much time with his youngest niece as he did with the older siblings.

On her feet again, the stranger extended her hand. "I'm Ginnie Ummarino."

"I can't thank you enough for taking care of her."

Ginnie bobbed her head. "I'm going to guess since you and I look nothing alike, it was the yellow dress that confused her."

His sister looked down at herself, as if she'd forgotten what she'd put on to wear that day.

"Oh, good." Alan approached from the opposite direction. The place was starting to sound like a broken record. "Looks like we're going to have to use the stroller on board or she'll find herself halfway to Kansas when we're not looking." The guy had a pretty good sense of humor. At least Nick's sister thought so as she leaned over and kissed her new husband's cheek.

The way those two looked at each other, Nick was surprised they didn't self combust, and once again he had to ask himself, why not leave the kids home with the grandparents for your honeymoon?

"Sorry." Theresa blushed. "This is my husband Alan."

"How do you do?" Alan extended his hand and

Phoebe's rescuer politely nodded.

"And these are our boys—" Theresa started, but the lady biting back a smile cut her off.

"Would I be too far off if I guessed, Chandler and Joey?"

Alan rolled his eyes and sighed. "Thankfully, no. Jake and Jeff."

"Sorry, I couldn't stop myself." Ginnie smiled bashfully.

"No worries," Theresa chuckled. "I probably shouldn't have watched so many episodes of *Friends*."

Grinning to himself over the sitcom-worthy gathering of relatives, Nick turned his attention from all the family that had appeared, to the lady who had sort of rescued Phoebe. Her smile was so delicate and her eyes reminded him of caramel candies. Funny, he was usually partial to light eyes, but something about this woman's gaze had him pulled in like a magnet to true north. Shaking his head, he brushed away the silly thoughts and returned his attention to the crazy crew he was supposed to help corral for the next eight days. "I hear there's ice cream somewhere on this ship. I think we've all earned it."

"On deck twelve. Take a left from the elevator. That's the closest self-serve soft ice cream machine," Ginnie volunteered.

"Thank you," Theresa offered and Nick found himself wanting to invite the lady with the warm brown eyes to join them.

Unfortunately, he had a job to do, and obviously he was going to have to step up his game if he wanted to keep tabs on all five kids. Pity, he would really have loved some time to get to know Miss Brown Eyes better.

CHAPTER THREE

The sun peeked through a narrow slit in the curtains. Just enough to tell Ginnie it was time to get out of bed. If that wasn't enough, her stomach rumbled loudly, begging to be fed. She'd spent yesterday, her first day at sea, relaxing in the upper lounge with a book and view to die for. Sipping iced tea while nibbling on a plate of cheese, crackers, and fruit had made the book even more enjoyable. So much so that dinner time came around and she'd barely had time to change out of her shorts and into something more appropriate.

For her, the large and ornate dining rooms were especially inviting. Maybe it was because the dining room in the house she'd shared with her sisters had been converted to an office long ago, or perhaps it had more to do with her Italian heritage and her mother's love of crushed velvet and massive furniture. Either way, she'd settled in at a table for eight. A mixed group at the table, the conversation had been steady, but nothing to get overly excited about.

Rather than dress and fight the crowds no doubt roaming about the upper deck before disembarking for the first island stop, she opted to wait for the majority of folks to disembark. To her delight, looking over the paperwork that came with her travel package, she realized that her company had included a few extra perks. The one she was most excited about was the gift card for the spa. Looking over the services, the massages sounded heavenly. Since she'd already been to today's port on both of her previous cruises, the idea of a good foot rub held way more appeal than a bus ride to ancient ruins.

Besides, this port required the ship drop anchor and the passengers tender into town. While she didn't mind riding the small crafts into the port, the lines and delays to come back at the end of the day were long, slow moving, and tiresome. Nope. A good hand, neck, and foot massage was the perfect plan for the day.

The need to hurry up kept nipping at her heels, urging her to get out the door sooner than later. Every few minutes she had to remind herself she was not at home, she didn't have to beat the traffic, find a parking space, wait for the elevator. This was a vacation and she could eat breakfast any time she wanted. Looking in the mirror, she pinned her hair up on top of her head, thankful that wearing makeup and high heels were not part of the cruise ship morning dress code.

Stepping into her new kitten heel sandals, she reached for the lanyard she'd bought on the last cruise since carrying her keycard in a pocket or purse wasn't very practical. The lanyard was efficient and pretty. Slipping it over her neck, she was ready to go. Taking one last look at herself in the mirror, not that anyone else would be looking, she nodded and headed out the door. Not more than two steps out, she realized she'd forgotten her coupon and stuttered to a stop, spinning in place, reached for her card, tugging too hard snapped the lanyard off, dropping it on the floor.

Squatting down, she grabbed the plastic portion that held the room keycard and it broke off from the lanyard. If this was a sign of how the rest of her day would go, maybe she should stay in her room. Keycard and broken lanyard in hand, she pushed to her feet but instead of rising, teetering on the new heels, she tipped back, arms flailing, wavering like a bobble toy, then landed on her derriere. Definitely should reconsider ordering room service for breakfast.

"Need some help?"

There was no need to look up, she recognized the smooth timbre of the voice from yesterday.

"Hi." Shaking her head, she leaned forward and pushed to her feet, praying she wouldn't topple forward and make more of a fool of herself. "And, no, thank you."

Nick—funny, she'd remembered his name—bobbed his chin, smiled, and took a step back.

Had he smiled the other day? He mustn't have or surely she would have noticed the dazzle that made her want to stare like a star-struck schoolgirl. "Are you on this deck?" She almost rolled her eyes at the stupid question. Why would he be here if his room weren't. Way to go, Ginnie.

"No." He shook his head, and held up the tall cup of specialty coffee in his hand. "I'm a couple of decks up, but the lines for the elevators and the crowds on the stairways is nuts. Decided to take a shortcut to the front of the ship in hopes that the other elevators will be less crowded."

"Good idea. That's always the case. Wherever the food is, so are the crowds. Though there will be a good number of folks hitting the buffet on that side than the dining rooms on this side, it should be less crowded."

"That sounds like the voice of experience. You sail a lot?"

Did two cruises count as a lot? "I've sailed before a couple of times, but not a lot."

He looked down the hall, but didn't move. Nodding again, he heaved a deep sigh. "I'd better get going before my mom is overrun by children."

After the whirlwind introductions the other day, she'd missed whose mother the older woman was. Between the five kids and four adults, she wasn't sure what the situation was, but at least now she knew he was related to the grandmother. "Kids' mom sleeping in?"

"No. My sister and her new husband were probably first off the ship this morning."

"New husband?" That might explain the blushing, but not the five children.

"Very new. This is their honeymoon."

"Really?" She shouldn't have said that out loud but trying to connect the dots with all the names and all the kids, a honeymoon scenario hadn't occurred to her, and at this hour with no coffee, her normal filters weren't kicking in yet.

"I know, but my mother keeps reminding me that even

the Brady's took their kids with them on their honeymoon."

If he was referring to the television show, his mom was right.

"Well," he raised the arm holding the coffee cup toward the end of the hall, "I really need to get going. It was nice seeing you again."

All she did was nod. It was nice seeing him again. Now all she wanted to know was if there was a Mrs. Smooth Voice to go with the mother and sister and new brother-in-law?

Nick had come within inches of asking Ginnie to join him on deck for a stroll and maybe a cup of coffee. Besides his knowing that by now some, if not all, of the kids were probably awake and his mother would be overwhelmed, just because she was alone outside her door didn't mean there wasn't a Mr. Brown Eyes. The guy could be inside sleeping or upstairs waiting for her for breakfast. Though if Nick were married to a looker like her, he would never leave her alone in a hall.

Pressing the button for the elevator, he was almost a little surprised when the doors opened and there was room for him inside. Ginnie had been right. In a fraction of the time it had taken him to get from the coffee shop to the hallway where Ginnie's room was, he'd made it across the ship, up the elevator and to their suite. No doubt anyone who walked by and saw the "Honeymoon Suite" sign on the door probably wondered why the heck would a family of nine need a honeymoon suite. He'd actually been a little surprised himself when he'd seen the sign. Apparently, knowing that Theresa and Alan were honeymooners, the staff had taken it upon themselves to change the sign on the multi-bedroom presidential suite to honeymoon suite. At least for this cruise. The ship had also left a chilled bottle of champagne and a large dish of chocolate-covered strawberries. All of which had been quickly scooped up and carried off to Theresa and Alan's room.

Pushing the door open, the silence surprised him. His mom sat on the sofa, a book on her lap, and a tall glass of lemon water. He'd forgotten how many years ago she gave up coffee and switched to lemon water in the morning, something her great aunt Delores had told her was the secret to longevity. "The kids are still sleeping?"

His mother closed her book. "The boys are. I think the girls are coloring quietly."

Coloring? Maybe this wasn't going to be as crazy a trip as he'd expected. "And Phoebe?"

"She's definitely awake, I can hear her talking to her toys, but she won't fuss as long as the draping is over the portable crib. I thought I'd wait for you then go in and get her up, change her diaper."

Better his mother than him. Though he'd gotten pretty good at diapers over the years, it was never his favorite thing. Especially the stinky ones. "So," he sat beside her on the sofa, "what's the plan for today?"

"Kids Club." His mother smiled. "There will be all sorts of things to keep the children happy till we get them for lunch."

"Then give them back?" Not that he didn't like his nieces, but he was willing to admit that four kids under twelve was a new experience for Uncle Nick and his sister and her husband weren't due back till after dinner.

"You bet. I think there's a movie after dinner for the older kids. I'll stay in with Phoebe if you want to go out and socialize with the adults."

Socializing with strangers didn't bother him, he was at least a bit of an extrovert, but that wasn't why he was here. He'd agreed to fill in for his dad, and his dad would not leave his mother home with the grandkids so he could hang out with other passengers. Even if one of them might be Ginnie.

The door to the boys' room creaked open and Jake came out first, yawning, followed by his younger brother Jeff. That was another pet peeve of Nick's. Why did parents have to name all their kids with the same first letter? Wasn't it hard enough to remember names, never mind when they all start with J or S or P or whatever?

Each boy sat at either side of Nick's mom, the sweet gesture tugging a smile out of her. Alan's parents had died one after the other several years ago so the boys didn't really have a grandmother and had taken to their new grandmother like white on rice.

"Hungry?" his mother asked.

Both heads bobbed, and within seconds, the girls' door opened. The noise level instantly rose in the suite. His mom was like a drill sergeant. Within minutes, all five kids were dressed, including Phoebe, and ready to head upstairs for breakfast. There was definitely an advantage to corralling hungry kids. They might be a bit whinier than usual, but they also eagerly dived into their food without making more work for supervising adults. So happy with their chocolate chip pancakes or whipped cream covered French toast, the kids didn't even seem to notice that the boat had begun rocking or the sun was sliding behind a stream of not so pretty-looking clouds.

The more the boat rocked, the more often his mother glanced in his direction. When the water began sloshing over the full glasses on the table, the casual glances from his mother had become filled with concern.

Glancing at his watch, Nick tossed his napkin on the table, and pushed his seat back. "Kids Club is open. We should make our way over." He didn't want to admit that it might take more time to get where they were going with the boat rocking so much. Whether or not it was indicative of anything or just a normal part of sailing on a cloudy day, Nick had no idea, but either way, the kids would have more fun involved in games with other kids than hanging out with two older people watching the windows, the storm, and wondering if the island was being hit as badly as the ship.

"Last one there is a rotten egg!" Jake cheered with three kids barreling after him.

"No running in the halls," his mom called after them.

Nick had opted to carry Phoebe in order to keep up with the kids who weren't quite running any longer but were moving pretty darn close to it.

The ship tilted left and his mother banged into the wall. "You okay?"

She nodded, shrugged, and kept walking. The kids were totally oblivious to the ship's movement. Maybe they should all almost run down the halls.

At the club, there were fewer kids than he had expected. The staff pointed out that many of the kids were on the island with their parents, if this were an at sea day, the place would be packed. Made sense to him. Immediately, the kids ran inside and each found something of interest and within minutes it looked to him like they were already making new friends.

With Phoebe in one arm and using his other arm to get him back down the hall, Nick kept an eye on his mom, leaning left and right in front of him like a Friday night drunk. If it was normal for a ship to rock harder than a mechanical bull, why in the heck did people keep coming back?

CHAPTER FOUR

I f Ginnie had ever been more relaxed, she had no idea when it could have been. Despite almost sliding off the massage chair near the end, twice, she still felt like she'd spent the last hour in heaven. Beyond any doubt, she was most definitely doing this again before the cruise ended.

"Be careful," the receptionist waved to her as she passed the front desk and reached the spa doors.

"Thank you." She wasn't sure what she was thanking the woman for, or why Ginnie needed to be told to be careful, but maybe that was something they told every passenger who walked out of the spa with limbs as relaxed as rubber bands.

All she wanted to do now was lie down and maybe read a good book, but somehow, doing that in her room felt wrong. With most of the passengers on the island, there were probably plenty of lounge chairs available on deck to enjoy her latest novel and soak up some vitamin D.

The ship lurched left and she bumped against the nearest wall. That was odd. Making her way to the double door to the deck, she stepped outside, the cool wind slapping her in the face. Since when was the wind on a cruise ship cool? Except maybe for an Alaskan cruise and last time she looked, they were in the wrong part of the ocean for that. Intent on crossing the ship to the elevator nearest her room, she reached an open deck and the gray skies immediately caught her eye. "Oh, that does not look good."

Now she needed to decide did she really want to try and cross the deck? Several staff were frantically scrambling around, stacking lounge chairs. Every so many seconds the ship would tip to one side and people would lose their footing or bump into the stacks. If folks who worked on this ship couldn't keep their balance, even if the railing was too high to fall over, she was not taking any chances. Turning around, she fought her way through the wind trying to push her back inside, and suddenly reading a book in one of the lounges sounded like a much better idea than on the sunless deck.

By the time she returned to her room and emerged from her cabin with her latest novel in hand, and her keycard and phone in the pouch dangling from her neck, everyone she passed on her way to her favorite lounge was muttering and most were bouncing off the walls like a pinball machine. She was rather proud of herself, she seemed to have found her sea legs. Wobbling a bit, but for the most part she was holding her own.

No sooner had she settled into a seat by the piano bar, when she could have sworn she heard a clunking sound. A heavy clunking sound. Curiosity aroused, she paused and listened carefully. The sound continued and her very relaxed muscles tightened. That was the anchor. Wasn't it? That or the ship was breaking apart with every smack of the growing waves. Neither option struck her as ideal.

Staring at the waves rolling higher and higher, Ginnie debated if she should worry. Part of her wanted to rely on every loud and frantic nerve of her Italian upbringing and run from the lounge screaming, while another part carefully reminded her that she'd never heard of a modern-day cruise ship sinking. She was still debating with herself when she noticed little Phoebe waddling her way at the end of her uncle's arm.

"Hello," the deep male voice called to her from several yards away.

"Hi." She closed the book she wasn't reading anyhow, and smiled at him.

The moment Phoebe spotted her, the little cherub grinned and seemed to be pulling her uncle behind her. The ship or the seas, or some combination thereof, must have known Phoebe was walking because for the first time since Ginnie had left the spa, the ship barely moved. When the child reached her, she flung her arms up at Ginnie.

Without any hesitation, Ginnie scooped the little one up. "Don't you look pretty today?"

Phoebe repeated what sounded like *petey.*

While Phoebe reached for the colorful stone hanging from Ginnie's necklace, Ginnie looked over Phoebe's shoulder. "Where's everyone else?"

"Mom's in the ladies' room and the other kids are in the ship's Kids Club. We were just on our way to check on how things are going with them. It's almost lunchtime and we didn't know if the weather was affecting their fun or not."

"My recollection of childhood is that very little interferes with having fun. They're probably oblivious." The words had no sooner left her lips than the ship did a severe tilt to one side and Ginnie had to do some fast footwork to keep from toppling over, Phoebe and all.

"Are sailings always this rough?" Those beautiful blue eyes narrowed.

Ginnie shook her head. "Not even close. I'm not sure what's going on, but I thought I heard the anchor moving."

"Moving?" Nick turned his gaze to the windows across the lounge. "As in going down or coming up?"

"They may have needed more length to avoid stress?" What she knew about ships, anchors, and physics wouldn't fill a thimble, but that was her best practical guess.

Nick's gaze shifted to the entryway at either side of the lounge. "I'd have thought Mom would have been here by now."

"Ladies and gentlemen." The deep voice over the loudspeaker cut off the elevator music that had been filtering through the ship. "I'm sure you've noticed the unexpected storm that has moved in."

"We'd have to be blind and stupid not to have noticed," Ginnie muttered.

"Agreed." Nick almost chuckled.

"Unfortunately, this storm is only going to get worse before it gets better. Remaining anchored is not best for the ship or the safety of the passengers. As a result, we've had no choice but to pull anchor and sail as quickly as we can out to sea in an effort to bypass the storm."

"He does mean after we load all the passengers in port, doesn't he?" Nick's gaze darted to the doorways again.

"Since it is not safe for the tenders to sail back to shore, all passengers in port will be housed until weather permits them to be transported to meet the ship at the next available port."

Nick's jaw dropped, his gaze shot to Phoebe before shaking his head. "This is so not good."

"Excuse me." An officer approached them. "Are you Mr. Maroney?"

"I am."

"Your mother said we'd find you here. I'm afraid she's had a little accident."

"What?" Nick sprang to his feet.

If she thought Nick's eyes had widened at the captain's announcement, right now his eyeballs looked ready to fall out of their sockets.

The officer lifted his hand. "She's perfectly all right, except she's injured her left ankle."

Ginnie looked from the dark and stormy water outside the wall of glass windows, to Phoebe, grinning up at her. Right about now, little Phoebe might be the only happy person on this ship.

Panic quickly surged through every blood vessel in Nick's body. "Where is my mother?"

"She's in the infirmary. I just happened to be coming out of the elevator when the ship rocked and she tripped down the stairs."

"She fell down the stairs?" Could this get any worse?

"Just a few steps. She was trying to avoid a couple of teens running up and just as she stepped down, the ship went left, she went right, and her foot snapped out from under her. The doctor is taking x-rays now, but she's more worried about you than herself."

"Can we see her?" Nick reached for Phoebe but his precious niece latched more tightly onto Ginnie.

"Yes. I'll be glad to take you to the infirmary."

Nick tried to coax Phoebe away from her newfound friend.

"Why don't we all go?" Ginnie shifted Phoebe to her other hip.

The only one in the group smiling was his niece. The last thing he needed was for the little girl to start screaming if he insisted on separating her from Ginnie. "If you don't mind."

Ginnie smiled and followed the two men out of the lounge, into the elevator and down a narrow hall below deck. All sorts of things were scurrying around in his mind. How badly was his mother really hurt, how could he reach his sister and her new husband, how long before they could rejoin the ship, how were the other kids doing at the Kids Club, and how amazing Ginnie was to step in and care for a clingy Phoebe.

"Hello, dear." His mom looked awfully pale.

"There are easier ways to ditch me." He snatched his mother's hand. "Why were you coming down the stairs? You went into the bathroom outside the lounge."

"The bathroom was being cleaned so I went to the one on the next floor up. I should have waited for the elevator, but I didn't want to keep you waiting."

"Do we know anything more?" He waved his chin at his mom's foot.

Just then, the ship's doctor came through a doorway. "Hello."

Everyone nodded at the man.

"I have good news. Nothing is broken."

His mother heaved a sigh and smiled. "I'll be honest, when I landed by this nice man and couldn't feel my ankle, I feared the worst."

"Well, there's a caveat to the good news."

Nick didn't like the sound of that.

"Soft tissue damage can take longer to heal than a clean break or fracture."

"Pft." Grimacing, his mother pushed on her hands to lift herself higher on the hospital bed. "A little ice and a few aspirin and I'll be good as new."

The doctor looked at Nick and he knew from the man's eyes that good as new was not going to be anywhere in his mother's immediate future.

"We're going to wrap the ankle for now. You'll need to ice it off and on for the next forty-eight hours. The faster the swelling decreases, the faster your ankle will heal, but that means it needs to be elevated higher than your heart."

"Fine." His mother leaned back. "Let's wrap this up, and send me on my merry way."

As if his mother had summoned her, a nurse came in with a tray and setting it down, removed the wrapping from an elastic bandage. The way his mom grit her teeth when the nurse touched the injured ankle, he knew beyond any doubt that she would not be up and about anytime soon.

"We have crutches, but the way the ship is rocking, it's probably best if you use one of our wheelchairs to return to your room." The doctor addressed the two of them.

Nick's "thank you," tumbled over his mother's "I can walk."

Both he and the doctor gave his mother a pointed glare.

His mom's mouth opened, no doubt ready to argue, when Ginnie stepped forward. "I bet Phoebe would love a ride on her grandmother's lap."

The way his mom snapped her mouth shut and blinked, Nick was willing to bet that for at least a few moments, she'd forgotten there were other people in the room.

Another staff member was already coming in with a wheelchair. His mom looked at it, looked at her ankle, then looked at Phoebe and nodded. "We'll make it a fun ride."

With a little encouraging from Ginnie, Phoebe settled into her grandmother's lap and he rolled his mom out the door. At the elevator, he turned to Ginnie. "Thank you."

Nodding, she softly responded, "You're going to need someone to hold Phoebe while you settle your mother in."

He'd already suspected this woman was beautiful both in and out, now he was positive. "If that's an offer, I accept."

A grin spread across her face. It was an awfully pretty smile. Not that he wished harm on his mother, but if she had to pick a place to mess up her ankle, she couldn't have picked a better time and place to do it. *Way to go, Mom.*

CHAPTER FIVE

All it took for Ginnie to see that Nick's mother was not going to be running a marathon anytime soon was about thirty seconds. If nearly collapsing in Nick's arms as she tried to stand out of the wheelchair wasn't enough, the pained grimace on her face as she panted away the pain was a dead giveaway.

"Some aspirin and a good night's rest and I'll be fine."

Nick hadn't bothered to say a word, he merely raised a brow at his mother and sighed. "Let's start by getting you comfortable." Before his mother could agree or disagree, Nick had scooped her into his arms and carried her to the sofa. "Here or the bedroom?"

Her lips pulled tightly together, whether in pain or frustration was anyone's guess. "Sofa. I want to be available for the kids."

"Are you sure? They won't be back for hours." On the way back to the suite they had stopped to get the kids for lunch, but the Kids Club provided lunch for those who wanted to stay, and all four kids were having too much fun to leave with the old people.

"I'm sure. Put me down before you hurt yourself."

Not wanting to juggle a toddler and pillows, and balance from the still rocking ship, Ginnie spied a few toys by the coffee table and set Phoebe down. Instantly the little girl reached for a big car and grinning broadly, started rushing it back and forth across the narrow table.

"Have we heard anything about Theresa and Alan?" His mother shifted on the sofa.

"Nothing. I thought I'd go check with the concierge after you're settled."

His mom sighed. "I'm settled. Go ask."

Nick shook his head. "A few more minutes isn't going to change anything."

"What do you need?" Ginnie asked.

His mother sighed. "I suppose if I'm not going to be walking any time soon, my puzzle book and glasses."

"Which is your room?" Ginnie asked Mrs. Maroney.

"Right there." Barely lifting her arm, she pointed to the room closest to the balconies.

Taking advantage of Phoebe's distraction, Ginnie went into the woman's room and grabbed eyeglasses and a crossword puzzle book from the night table. Her next objective while Nick gathered pillows was ice. Except no refrigerator. Scanning the suite, she spotted an ice bucket. Perfect. She'd lifted the lid, surprised to find the bucket already filled. She'd have loved a plastic bag, but for now, hand towels would do.

Another couple of minutes and Ginnie had the puzzle book and glasses at Mrs. Maroney's side, and stood next to Nick. "That's not high enough."

Nick looked at her as if she'd grown a second head or a third boob or both.

"Her ankle needs to be above her heart and iced on and off every twenty minutes," she reminded him of what the doctor had said, handing him the ice packs.

His gaze traveled from his mother's chest to her foot and sighing, he bobbed his head. "Right. One more cushion should do it."

While Nick finished setting his mother up, Ginnie shifted her attention to Phoebe. Incredibly well behaved, the kid had to be at least a little hungry. On a shelving unit that had been set up as a kitchen counter, she spotted bread and peanut butter. On a whim, she checked the mini bar. Sure enough, Theresa had put jelly in there. Peanut butter and jelly sandwiches had to be the American mom's go to easy meal for little kids on a road trip, and cruises were basically glorified road trips.

By the time Nick had his mother comfortably settled in with her ankle propped up on multiple pillows, Phoebe was happily sitting on the floor by the coffee table, eating her sandwich sections with one hand and her other hand still playing with the cars, oblivious to the ship's constant movement.

Ginnie was pretty proud of herself. The advantage of coming from a big family was that there was always a little kid around who belonged to someone, and pretty much every member of the family knew how to care for them. Babysitters were always needed and teenage relatives were always available. "What's Phoebe's nap time?"

"Usually noon," Mrs. Maroney replied. "Once she's done with her sandwich she can be put down. We turn on the sound machine and cover the portable bed and she should sleep for hours."

"Good sleeper." Ginnie nodded.

Mrs. Maroney grinned as if Ginnie had just announced the woman's grandchildren were all prodigies. "All of Theresa's girls were good sleepers. My daughter read a book. I hated that she put more faith in the book than in me, but the kids have a great sleep routine that works anywhere."

Ginnie made a mental note to talk to Theresa about what book she'd used. There was more than one cousin in the family who lamented needing a good night's sleep or a break in their day from infants or young toddlers who didn't want to nap or sleep at night. Then she should probably find a spare minute to phone her family in case the ship's situation made the news, but for now, helping with Phoebe and Nick's mom came first.

While Nick cleaned up Phoebe's hands and mouth and readied her for naptime, Ginnie called for another bucket of fresh ice. In another few minutes, the new ice bucket was in the mini fridge and Phoebe was down for the count.

"What would you like me to order for you for lunch?" Nick asked his mom.

The woman shook her head. "You know I don't eat lunch. Not unless I want to gain a few pounds a day."

The way Nick rolled his eyes, Ginnie had the feeling he and his mother had been reliving an established conversation.

"You two, on the other hand," his mother continued, "must be starving. See what you can find out about your sister and then get something decent to eat at a sit-down establishment."

Nick's lips pressed into a thin line as he considered his mother's suggestion. "I'd rather not leave you alone."

"Oh, don't be silly." His mother waved him off. "The wheelchair is right here in case I need to see a man about a horse. The bathroom in my room is bigger than the one in my house. I'll be fine. And if push comes to shove, I can give Phoebe another ride in my lap."

The way his mother smiled at him, Ginnie saw something that reminded her of her aunt Antonia. Mrs. Maroney could probably handle Phoebe and a few more kids, if she had to, on one leg with her arm tied behind her back.

"Go," his mother repeated.

"Fine." Nick took a step in retreat. "But we'll be back before Phoebe wakes up."

"Fair enough." His mother shifted ever so slightly and began working her crossword puzzles. No doubt pleased to have won this round.

There was only one thing about how this day was playing out that Nick liked: a chance to get to know Ginnie better. Aside from that, everything was falling apart at the seams. The ship was moving along, but still swaying from side to side. Any minute now he expected to see chairs and tables and dishes and maybe even people flying back and forth like a scene from a bad tornado movie.

"Has your sister tried to reach you?" Ginnie walked slowly at his side.

In all the chaos of the announcement and his mother's fall, it hadn't occurred to him to look at his phone.

"I thought I overheard the passenger entering the room across the hall say something about the ship turning on phone access to all passengers because folks were left behind."

Enthused for all of three seconds, he immediately noticed only one bar on his phone. "The ship may have given us access, but the storm seems to have other ideas." He flipped his phone around for her to see.

"Maybe when we get away from this mess you'll be able to talk to your sister."

"Hope so. I'd feel better if I knew they were somewhere comfortable and safe." He didn't want to share all the visions of past tsunamis and hurricane images that were replaying in his mind.

"I'm sure they're fine." Her lips tipped up at the corners and a sparkle shone in her eyes. "Probably enjoying time alone."

He couldn't argue with that. "If you don't mind, I'd like to hit the concierge desk before grabbing a bite to eat."

"Don't mind at all. I'd like to find out how long before they think we'll be able to sail out of this mess and when the other passengers will be able to join us."

Once they reached the promenade deck, he was surprised by how few passengers were milling about. Then, as if to remind him, the ship leaned sharply left, almost knocking him and Ginnie off their feet. Smart people were probably in their cabins and not trying to walk around.

As they approached a café, a young woman with long blonde hair sat like a rag doll in one of the chairs. Her head tipped back along the top of the seat, her companion had a cloth he was dipping in a water glass and gently wiping her forehead. His face pinched with concern, he softly asked her if she thought she could make it back to the room. The poor woman started to shake her head and stopping short, her one hand flew to her stomach and the other to her mouth.

Now that Nick looked a little more closely, the poor woman did appear a bit green around the gills. The ship shifted again and once more, Ginnie bounced against him. This time he grabbed her by the arms to steady them both. "You okay?"

Her gaze locked with his and she dipped her chin just a

hint. For a long moment neither moved until the ship swayed in the opposite direction and Nick jogged back a few steps.

Ginnie stretched out an arm to balance herself against the shop window. "I think we rock less when we keep moving."

"Agreed. Let's get moving." He almost reached out and grabbed her hand. The move felt so natural, but common sense prevailed.

"Oh, dear." She stuttered to a halt.

Nick glanced up in the direction she stared. A line of people at the concierge desk wrapped around the atrium and down the opposite hall. He bit his tongue, because what he was thinking wasn't as fitting for polite company as *oh, dear*. "Maybe we need to eat now and ask questions later."

"Or maybe you need to get in line and I need to go bring us back a hot dog or something easy to eat while standing."

For a fraction of a moment he considered her suggestion, then he looked at the length of the line and knew it wasn't going anywhere anytime soon. "No, let's get some food. Maybe they'll make a general announcement soon."

"Ladies and gentlemen, this is the captain speaking." He hadn't needed to announce who he was, Nick remembered the voice from earlier and couldn't help but think what perfect timing. "We have no solid information for you on when the storm will pass or when your fellow passengers and loved ones will be able to rejoin the ship. Please be patient and we will update you as soon as we have more information to share."

There was lots of muttering and some people on the line shifted about.

"I am guessing in about five minutes' half of those people are going to realize they're hungry and aren't going to learn anything more when they get to the front of the line."

A handful of people stepped out of the line and Nick knew she was right. "But I don't think they're going to need even five minutes." Spinning around, he grabbed the hand he'd wanted to grab early and darted towards the rear elevators leading up to the buffet. "Last man to the elevator is a rotten egg."

The loud cackle that escaped Ginnie's throat made his bold gesture of grabbing her hand and bolting down the ship so totally worth it.

CHAPTER SIX

For the first time in forever, Ginnie felt like a schoolgirl. Running through the ship, holding hands with a good-looking guy, skirting around people lingering on the shopping deck, bumping into each other when the ship rocked. The laughter only grew louder and stronger. As if propelled by rocket fuel, they darted up the stairs. With each flight, their steps slowing ever so slightly. When a couple of teens came racing up the stairs halfway to the buffet deck, their gazes caught, his grip on her tightened, and with only a sly smile, the two raced the kids up the rest of the stairs—and won!

Of course, at the top of the stairs breathing was coming hard and heavy, but they'd done it, and even if her lungs were desperate for air, she couldn't stop laughing. "That was fun."

Sucking in a long deep breath, bending over in a mirror image of her stance, one hand on his knee, the other still holding onto her, Nick nodded. "It was, wasn't it?" He lifted his head to where the kids were now running across the floor and into the buffet area. "But I might need to be in better shape if we're going to do this again."

That only made her laugh harder. "Maybe I'll just have a salad for lunch."

"Salads are good for rabbits." Nick straightened and tugged at her hand. "We'd better get moving or the crowds will beat us."

She almost winced when Nick let go of her hand. She wasn't sure he'd realized how long he'd been holding it. And she wasn't sure why she felt so comfortable with her hand in his. Many a date, with guys she'd known well, had been spent avoiding contact like that, and yet, everything about that last few minutes felt so very normal. If her sisters knew what she was thinking, they'd be rolling with laughter too. Ginnie was the practical sister, and she never, ever ran, for any reason. Not even in school. She was very much allergic to sports and exercise. So why did she have an overwhelming urge to familiarize herself with the ship's gym?

Inside the buffet area, they grabbed a plate, went through the line, and Nick led the way toward the wall of glass. "How's this?"

"Perfect." She loved a table with a view.

Settling into her seat, she realized she'd forgotten to grab a knife. Pushing her chair back, she stood and stopped. "Where did all these people come from?"

Nick turned toward all the tables and let out a short laugh. "Looks like we beat the crowds by a hair."

From the looks of it, every soul in line downstairs must have made their way to food. The few tables left empty were quickly filling up and there were more people mulling about the food stations. Another minute and she was back in her seat and ready to dig into the beef and broccoli. The baked ziti had been tempting, but after running up the stairs she opted for anything that resembled protein and vegetables.

"How is it?" Nick watched her dig into her meal.

Swallowing quickly, she nodded. "Pretty good. The food rarely disappoints. It might not be worth writing home over, but it's always tasty."

"You mentioned you'd sailed… was it twice?"

He remembered. "That's right. The first time we came when our neighbor's husband was deployed unexpectedly and gave us their tickets. None of us had sailed before."

"Us?"

"My sisters and me. There was a little snafu with the reservations. Long story short, we wound up in a suite and my sister Mina met her now husband."

"Nice perk for a snafu."

"She thinks so. Next cruise was with my sisters again

for her bachelorette trip."

"Mina or another sister?"

"The trip was for Mina, but as it turns out, my younger sister Jo met her now husband on that cruise."

"No more siblings to travel with?"

She shook her head. "I won this trip from my company. This was the last cruise before the award expired, and neither of my sisters could get away."

"So you decided alone was better than not at all?"

"Seemed like a good idea at the time. Everyone needs a little R&R from time to time. To unplug from this crazy world."

"I'm afraid we've invaded on your R&R. I'm sorry."

"Oh, no." Again she shook her head. "Your family has been a pleasant surprise. Phoebe is such a sweetie. Though I do feel badly about your mother, and hopefully you'll have word on your sister soon."

"Yeah." He glanced out the window at the gray skies. They were still surrounded by dark clouds and splashing rain, but he could see in the distance the sky was a shade or two lighter. "Hopefully, we'll all be in cell phone range soon."

"I'm sure she's fine."

His gaze met hers. "I hope so." He chuckled softly. "Actually, I hope that little island has enough hotel space for all the people. I think we had to have left more than half the ship."

"Good thing you came along with your mother to help. That was very nice of you."

"Not that nice. My dad was supposed to come but he came down with Covid after the wedding. Well, he probably had it during the wedding but we won't tell anyone that."

She shook her head and drew her hand across her mouth. "My lips are sealed."

Over lunch she heard more about how his sister lost her husband in a car crash and then almost immediately learned she was pregnant with their third child.

"It hit the whole family hard. Even though it feels like everyone has adjusted and moved along, whenever I see Monica practically strangling the stuffed bunny in her arms, I know things still aren't quite right."

"I don't think I follow. What's wrong with having a favorite stuffed toy?"

"Absolutely nothing. That toy in particular was the last gift Chuck gave Monica. Sometimes she hangs on to the thing as if it could bring her father home again."

"Oh, that is sad. Though I suspect it also gives her great comfort."

"I'm sure it does, but what do I know. I'm not a child psychologist, just an uncle."

"An uncle who cares."

"That I do." He nodded slowly, then heaving a soft sigh, leveled his gaze with hers. "Tell me more about your family."

Where to start explaining her big, crazy, Italian family? "In my house, if you forget someone's name, just call out Toni. Whether it's an Antonia, or Antoinette, or Antonio, they'll all answer to Toni."

That made him chuckle. "You don't roast goats in the front yard, do you?"

His reference to *My Big Fat Greek Wedding* had her chuckling again. Smiling and laughing was so easy around him. "No goats. No front yards. Plenty of back yards and lots and lots of pasta."

"I like pasta."

So did she, and unfortunately, so did her hips.

"There's still time till Phoebe wakes up. What do you say we hit the concierge again? See if there's more news."

"I suppose we could try."

His mouth suddenly dropped open and he shook his head. "I'm sorry. You've been so helpful, I forgot you might actually like to do something fun on your vacation."

"Oh, no. I mean, well, yes, that is, I'm glad to help out. I just don't think there's going to be much new information yet."

"Then I'd better get back and check on Mom and Phoebe."

"Yes." What she didn't know was if she was included in his plans or not. She was still considering what she should do next as they made their way down the stairs rather than wait for the elevator. If only he'd take hold of her hand again. She'd gladly follow him anywhere for the rest of the cruise.

How thoughtless of Nick to assume that Ginnie would want to continue spending time helping him corral his family and care for his mother. Having her at his side most of the morning had seemed so natural that he'd actually forgotten, they were practically strangers. Even though he barely knew her, somehow being around her felt more normal than being on a ship with his sister and her family. None of the usual awkwardness that creeps up when meeting someone new made an appearance. When he'd grabbed her hand earlier to beat the crowds to lunch, not till they'd reached the top of the stairs had he noticed he was still holding on to her. Letting go had taken way more effort than it probably should have.

On top of that, he had to fight the urge to reach out and cover her hand resting on the table. Now that they were out the door and on their way downstairs, he opted to put his hands in his pockets rather than snatch hold of hers again. She hadn't shown any objection the first time, but why push his luck.

Once they reached the correct deck, two of the cruise staff were parked in front of the main entrance to one of the many ship lounges. The female shifted to one side and holding on to a card, stopped in front of Ginnie while her male counterpart did the same to him.

"Here to play Bingo?" the young woman asked with a smile way bigger than it should have been for accosting strangers passing by.

"We're on our way to the front desk for any updates on the weather and the passengers left behind," Ginnie spoke up.

The young man shook his head. "There's nothing new. The passengers are being accommodated on the island and the weather is still with us."

Not what he'd wanted to hear. At least not the weather part, but he would have loved to have more specific information on his sister and her new husband.

"We're giving one free Bingo card to get you started." The young woman was still grinning.

"It's good for three games," the young man added. "And there are lots of fun prizes."

"Yes." Somehow the woman's smile grew larger. "There's a dinner at a specialty restaurant, several hundred dollar jackpots, and a day at the spa."

"Spa?" For the first time since they hit the landing, Ginnie looked interested.

Since he wasn't going to get any more info from the cruise line, his niece still had another hour or so to nap, and he didn't want to say goodbye to Ginnie, he looked at her and shrugged. "Want to give it a whirl?"

"What about your mom?"

"She's probably loving reading her book in peace and quiet."

Her grin blossomed. "Okay."

The front of the cruise ship's lounge was decorated with bright colorful banners. Two of the staff were set up at a table on the stage. In front of them a massive round cage filled with balls waited for the first spin. Through the lounge, other staff members offered more Bingo cards for sale, but they were content with their one card each.

Since they only had time for the one quick game, they both took a seat near the rear doors, making a quick exit easier.

Raising the microphone to her mouth, a young blonde with her hair pulled back in a ponytail that added to her youthful look, waved at a few people still coming in the door. "Welcome everyone to shipboard Bingo! Grab your cards, find a seat, and get ready for some fun!"

"She seems a tad overly enthusiastic for Bingo." Ginnie tipped her head. "Don't you think?"

"Now if you'll look more closely at your cards," the blonde kept talking, "you'll notice we've spiced the game up a bit."

Nick looked down. "S-P-I-C-Y?"

"Hmm." Ginnie lifted her gaze to the blonde still talking.

"The rules are the same as ordinary Bingo, when the letter and number are called out, mark it with the wipeable highlighters we gave you."

Pressing her lips into a tight line, Ginnie settle into her seat, clutched the marker and nodded.

"You take your games seriously, don't you?" he asked.

"Two sisters, big family, lots of egos. Yes. Besides, I want that spa day."

He bit back a smile. "Let's get it done."

As the pair of staffers alternated calling out a number, they diligently marked their cards. More missed numbers than matches.

"S 10," the blonde called out.

Ginnie bounced in her seat. "One more."

Her luck was doing better than his, he only had half a dozen matches.

Another number called and a woman with gray hair as high as she was wide sprang up. "Spicy!"

"Darn it," Ginnie muttered.

"Shall we do it again?"

Her one brow lifted and he was thankful he didn't blush easily as she sputtered a chuckle. "Sure."

Scrubbing the marks off with the microfiber towelettes handed out, Nick readied himself for the next round. When he finished he turned to Ginnie who, her card already cleaned off, leaned back and smiled at him. "Care for a private wager?"

His knee-jerk reaction was to say *you're on*, but another side of him paused a minute. Did he really want to compete with her?

"Chicken?" she teased.

"You're on." Who knew Bingo could be so fun?

"First one to get Bingo—"

"You mean Spicy…" he grinned.

"Right. Spicy. First one to complete their card gets a drink of their choice."

"I'm fond of bourbon, on the rocks." He smiled. "Just so you know."

The blonde announced the first number of the new game and Nick almost laughed at the intensity in Ginnie's deep brown eyes.

Another few minutes and this time a skinny woman who looked old enough to be everyone in the room's grandmother proudly shouted out, "Spicy!"

"Darn it," Ginnie muttered. "This is why I never play the lottery."

"One more?" He looked at her, watching his choice of words more carefully.

Ginnie nodded, and the blonde announced this next round was for the first one hundred dollar prize.

"S 21."

"Ooh, good start," Ginnie squealed and Nick resisted the urge to kiss the grin off her face.

More calls were made, and Nick marked up more numbers than in the previous two games combined.

"Oh, look. You only need one more." Her gaze fell on his card.

Even though he'd been marking away, he hadn't realized how close he was to Bingo, or Spicy.

Another wrong number and then another. This is why Nick preferred competitions of skill rather than chance.

One more number and marking her card quickly, Ginnie's eyes popped and mouth dropped before she sprang up shouting, "Spicy!" at the top of her lungs.

"Looks like we only have one winner." The blonde waved to another staffer to check the numbers. In about ten seconds, the young man nodded at the blonde. "Congratulations, you're our first hundred dollar winner!"

Ginnie spun around with the finesse of a ballerina and

threw her arms around him with the force of an Olympic athlete. Squeezing tightly, and staying in the fold of his arms, she leaned back and squealed even louder, "We won!"

She'd won the Bingo game, but as far as he was concerned, he was most definitely the winner for the day.

CHAPTER SEVEN

Pulling back from hugging Nick, she did her best to react as if embracing this near stranger was perfectly normal. Inching back, she smiled up at him and squealed, "I can't believe we won."

"You mean you won." Nick smiled. "And if you don't hurry up and collect, they may give it to someone else."

"They wouldn't dare." She chuckled and taking another step to the side, glanced down the lounge to the front and ignoring the new numbers they were calling, waved for Nick to follow her. For some reason she'd been expecting a gift card or shipboard credit, receiving an envelope with cash left her dumbfounded.

Nick appeared beside her smiling. "Looks like you're buying drinks even though you won."

"If I were home, I'd play the lottery." Tucking the envelope into her neck pouch, she moved her phone into her hip pocket and reminded herself that as soon as they had a signal she needed to call her family and let them know all was going well.

He shrugged sheepishly. "Maybe we should hit the casino?"

"Maybe." She wasn't going to mention she knew next to nothing about gambling. "For now, should we check in on the Kids Club?"

He shook his head. "I'd rather get back and check on Mom and Phoebe."

"Of course." Hesitating, she looked over his shoulder at the double exit doors and then leveled her gaze with his. "Would you like some help?"

"If you're offering…"

"I am."

"You sure?"

She nodded. Spending time with Nick and his family held much more appeal than snuggling up with a paperback novel.

"Then let's go."

For a fraction of a moment, she thought he was going to take hold of her hand again, but all he did was slip his hands into his pocket and lead the way across the ship to the family's suite.

Using the keycard in his short's pocket, Nick slowly shoved the door open.

"Back so soon?" his mother smiled up at them, setting her own paperback down on her lap.

Quickly crossing the room, he sat at his mom's side. "How are you doing?"

"Really well. Even managed to see a man about a horse."

The confusion on Ginnie's face must have been obvious, because Nick rolled his eyes and then softly chuckled. "That's Mom's favorite euphemism for the ladies' room."

"I see." She didn't. Why wouldn't she have just said bathroom, restroom, or ladies' room, but no reason to speak up now.

Nick's gaze shifted to the wheelchair still in the corner where they'd left it and his brows buckled. "How did you get there?" Immediately, his eyes flew open wide. "You didn't walk on it, did you?"

This time his mother rolled her eyes. "No." Then she smiled at him, lifting her chin, looking very proud of herself. "I hopped."

"Oh, Mom." She could hear his sigh from across the room. "You could have fallen and hurt yourself more."

"Oh, for heaven's sake. It's not like I joined the conga line on the pool deck."

Ginnie had to cover her mouth to hold back a chuckle.

"Mother!"

Now Ginnie bit on her cheeks. She could picture this

exact scenario between herself and her sisters with their mom. No matter where you were raised, some things simply didn't change.

"Oh, get off your high horse. I can hear Phoebe talking to herself again. She's probably ready to get up, and I could use some more ice. It's been a while."

"Do you want me to take care of Phoebe or the ice?" Ginnie asked.

Nick chuckled to himself. "I'll get Phoebe. You're too nice to make you change diapers."

Too nice. She didn't know if she should grin excitedly, or object to being spared a diaper change.

"That's my boy," his mom cheered. "While you're at it, dear, could I have a glass of water too? Carrying water and hopping do not go well together."

"Of course." She spun around and wrapped the ice before pouring a bottle of water into a glass. A few more minutes and his mother was all settled and Phoebe was grinning happily. For the next couple of hours, Ginnie and Nick were on the ground playing with little Phoebe, occasionally refreshing the ice for his mother's ankle, and everyone was relieved when they received a call from Theresa. As they suspected, the couple were enjoying the quaint hotel the ship had set them up in, even though the storm was still heavy over the port, the lovebirds didn't seem to care.

At one point when his mom rose to use the ladies' room again, Nick hurried to grab the wheelchair and wheel her to the bathroom. "No one is hopping around on my watch." After that, he arranged for his mother to have crutches for short trips.

The next thing she knew, with Phoebe on her hip, and Nick pushing his mother in the wheelchair, they were picking up four children from the Kids Club and fielding a plethora of squeals and stories and giggles and laughter and pleas to do the movie night.

The older boy, Jake, walked backward down the hall to the dining room. "Dad said that we didn't have to follow bedtime rules on the ship."

"He did, did he?" Nick stared at the kid while his mother nibbled on her lower lip in an effort not to smile.

"Yes," the second boy chimed in, now walking in reverse like his brother.

"Mom too." One of the girls spun about like the boys.

"Mommy said so," the other girl confirmed. Though Ginnie had the feeling that like her kid sister Jo, this little one would have sworn the sky was green if her sister said so.

Corralling the five kids and one mother in a wheelchair into the dining hall was a bit more lively than Ginnie had expected, though it shouldn't have been. The more she thought back to her own childhood, the more she realized what drama she and her two sisters had often caused her parents.

At one point, the boys decided tossing the bread was easier than passing it around. All Nick had to do was clear his throat for the boys to stop. Then there was the argument between the girls over whose napkin belonged to whom. The grandmother stepped in for that one, and Nick leaned into her. "I'm sorry about this. They're usually much better behaved."

"They're just being kids," she said softly enough that only Nick could hear.

With every childlike behavior, Nick would repeat the same apology, and she would reassure him. Apparently, he had no idea the ruckus her big Italian family could make over the littlest of things.

When dinner was over, the score was one for the kids and zero for Uncle Nick. They were all, except Phoebe, going to watch *Despicable Me 3* on deck with the rest of the Kids Club. The four pretty much skipped down the hall again, giddy with anticipation. She couldn't blame them. She'd be giddy too if she were going to watch a movie under the stars with a certain sweet and good-looking uncle. Wouldn't that be something?

Once again, his mother was comfortably settled in with an ice pack and her book. Only this time, in bed instead of on the sofa, and Phoebe was tucked snug as a bug in the proverbial rug, or in this case, crib. And once again, his mom had convinced them to go find something fun to do while the kids enjoyed the movie. Bless her.

For years, she'd been teasing and prodding for him to find a nice girl. She'd even tried to set him up a few times under some ridiculous guise. But this time, he could have hugged her if Ginnie hadn't been there watching.

"You're smiling."

"I am?"

Ginnie nodded. "You are. Want to share?"

"I was just remembering the time my mom invited a friend from work over for dinner."

"My mom loves having a full dinner table too."

"Except this one came with her single daughter, who my mother just knew I was going to fall madly in love with at first sight."

Ginnie spit out a laugh. "Ah, one of those dinners."

"You too?"

"It's gotten worse since my younger sister beat me to the altar." Shaking her head slightly and still smiling, she sighed. "I gather it was not love at first sight."

"Not even close. She was pretty enough, and smart enough, but all she could talk about was her work."

"Oh. What did she do?"

"An actuary."

Ginnie frowned. "As in, insurance algorithms?"

He bobbed his head. "Made for riveting dinner conversation."

"I can imagine," she giggled.

Oh, he was really liking the sound of her laughter. "What about you?"

"What about me?"

"What kind of men did your mother try and set you up with?"

"Italian."

"And?"

"No and. Just Italian. Tall ones, short ones, fat ones, skinny ones, smart ones, not so smart ones."

"Wow. Sounds like your mother is a little more ambitious than mine."

"Ambitious is one word for Mom. Stubborn, determined, and one of my favorite people in the world rounds her out."

"That's nice."

"What? That my mother is stubborn and ambitious?"

"That you love her so much."

She shrugged. "So do you."

"I didn't know I loved your mother." He tried not to laugh at his own stupid joke.

"Ha ha. You know what I meant."

"I do." He nodded. "And you're right. Mom is great, especially when she's not playing matchmaker."

"I think our mothers would be good friends."

"Why does that thought scare me?"

Ginnie laughed again. "Okay. Good point."

Her words were cut off with the sound of music. Until now he wasn't sure where they were going, just walking from the movie deck to the opposite side of the ship.

Her gaze wandered through the open doors into the nearby lounge. "Oh. It's karaoke."

"You like to sing?"

"Singing might not be the right word, but I enjoy hearing others."

Stopping, he bowed at the waist and waved his arm toward the double doors. "Then hearing others we shall do."

The small lounge was surprisingly full. It took a few minutes to find a seat, but they settled in.

"I owe you a drink." He waved down a waiter.

"I'll have a Marvelous Mango please." She spun about in the swivel chair. "Thanks."

"Hey." He shrugged. "That was the bet."

She nodded. "It was, but not everyone settles a bet."

"I may be many things, but a welcher isn't one of them."

"I'll remember that." Her grin was downright infectious.

With one hand on their hip and the other pointing at the audience, a very nice group of girlfriends, who couldn't carry a tune in a paper bag, sang the last line of "Shake It Off" to raucous applause.

"Maybe next time the audience should sing along," he teased, leaning into her side so no one else would hear.

A tall blonde with long flowing hair and a snug fit dress marched onto the stage. The way the woman grabbed the microphone and waited for her cue, without glancing at the karaoke screen, had Nick thinking this was not her first karaoke effort.

A few notes played and Ginnie smiled. "Ooh. I love this song."

"We've heard all of three notes and you recognize it?"

She bobbed her head. "I can name most Carrie Underwood tunes in less than that."

Another few notes and even Nick recognized the song "Before He Cheats."

"What do you think?" Ginnie leaned toward him. "All flash or can she really sing?"

He shrugged, and a moment later, all of three words, to match the three notes, came over the sound system and his and Ginnie's jaws dropped before quickly snapping shut.

"I'm guessing this is going to be very good." Ginnie leaned back in her seat. By the time the woman belted out the chorus, Ginnie was sitting up straight, shaking her head. "What a set of pipes."

"That about says it all. I have no idea how anyone is going to have the nerve to get up and sing after her."

When she finished, not only was there thunderous applause but several people had jumped to their feet. Nick couldn't blame them, he almost did the same.

"Wow."

It didn't take long for Nick to learn that very few people were discerning of their own skills. Not one, or two, but the next three singers were mediocre at best and couldn't have cared less. Especially an older brunette who was waving her arms with the rise in music as if she were guiding an aircraft at the airport into its gate.

The brunette left the stage to generous applause and this time a guy got on stage. From the way he walked up, his shoulders slightly slumped, Nick got the feeling the guy wasn't having a great time so far. His girlfriend or wife had probably coaxed him into this.

"He doesn't look too happy to be up there." Ginnie's gaze followed the man.

Nick nodded. "I was just thinking the same thing."

"I saw him at the jewelry store before Phoebe bumped into me. I noticed he didn't look happy then either." A few seconds later and the first notes of the song played and Ginnie bobbed her head. "This might explain the dour demeanor?"

"What?" He wasn't sure what she'd noticed. Nick actually glanced around for signs of something, what he didn't know.

"'Unbreak My Heart.' It's a Toni Braxton song and could explain a few things."

The guy belted out the song, and thankfully on key, because nothing could be worse than a sad song and a bad voice. Towards the end, Nick actually began to feel for the guy. There was just a little too much emotion in his rendition to just be a song.

The song over, the singer nodded and trudged off the stage.

"Poor guy," Ginnie's gaze tracked the guy walking to a table alone. "Hope he meets someone nice while on board."

Breaking into both their thoughts, one of the staff announced over the sound system, "We have plenty of slots. Come forward and pick your song."

"Not on your life," Ginnie muttered.

"Chicken?" he teased.

"Not going to work on me." She shook her head. "That which I do, I do well, and that which I don't do well, I delegate. I refuse to get up there and make a fool of myself."

He wondered if she really didn't sing well or was merely underestimating herself. Only one way to find out.

CHAPTER EIGHT

The man had clearly lost his mind. "You getting up there and making a fool of yourself isn't a good reason for me to do the same. As my mom used to say, 'If your friends jump off a bridge, are you going to follow?' My answer was always, 'No, Mama.' I can honestly say, my mama didn't raise any fools."

"Chicken."

"Don't you know any other words?" She did her best to glare at him, but her eyes held too much sparkle.

"Dare you. Those are two words."

"Nope." She was not falling for it. She had too much self esteem. Or maybe it was a healthy sense of self-preservation.

"I'll buy you another Marvelous Mango."

"Nope."

The next gentleman up had to be the weakest of all the evening's singers. To make matters worse, he didn't look all that comfortable up there either.

"See." Nick waved at the guy on stage. "Nobody can be worse than him."

"You got me there."

"Great. I'll see you on stage after I pick my song."

"Wait. What?" His back was already disappearing from view. She did not agree to sing, only that the poor guy on stage was lousy. Heaving out a sigh, she shook her head. Now what was she going to do?

Two more people came up to sing a duet of Sonny and Cher's "I Got You, Babe." That had to be one of the most sung karaoke songs in the world, right after "I Will Survive." At least these two weren't half bad. The woman had a stronger voice that drowned out her cohort. Maybe if Ginnie got up with Nick and just moved her lips, no one would notice. After all, the guy was pretty good-looking. At least all the women in the place would be watching him, not her.

The waiter retrieved her empty glass. "Would you like another drink?"

"Yes, thank you." She might need the liquid encouragement if she was really going to get up and do this. Was she? Closing her eyes, she shook her head at no one. Nope. There was no reason for her to punish the audience with her lack of vocal skills.

Signing for her drink, she recognized the first notes of one of her mother's favorite Michael Bublé songs, "Sway". Tipping the waiter more than she probably should, she smiled at the man and turned her attention to the stage. Good grief, Nick was standing, watching the screen with the lyrics, waiting for the right notes. Her heart skipped a beat and she'd swear her palms began to sweat.

She was more nervous for him than she would be for herself and yet, despite the anxiousness, she found her fingers tapping on the table's edge, waiting for his first note. By the time Nick got to the line about the ocean hugging the shore, her mouth hung wide open. His voice was absolutely magical. Every note resonated deep inside her.

When his eyes lifted and his gaze met hers, she sucked in a deep breath. His eyes were as dreamy as his voice. She couldn't help but smile up at him. Even if he wasn't really singing to her—after all, they'd never danced, heck, they technically barely knew each other—and yet, it felt like she was the only person in the room and he was singing directly to her. As long as the song lasted, she was going to savor this moment. Her toes tapped the same beat as her fingertips and one shoulder shifted up and down until she was doing exactly as the song said. Yes, she was savoring every note; later she could figure out a way to get out of making a fool of herself.

As Nick placed the microphone back into the stand, he glanced up one more time at Ginnie, up on her feet and clapping so hard her hands probably hurt. He wasn't really sure what made him pick that song, he'd been mulling over two or three other options when he spotted that song and instantly decided that was what he was going to sing.

The only downside was that all through the song he kept wishing he could walk out into the audience, take hold of Ginnie's hand, and dance with her. Now wasn't that ridiculous. There had been a lot of attractive, stunning, and seductive women who had crossed his path. He'd have had to be dumb and blind not to notice them, or want to get a little bit more up close and personal. But never had he wanted to simply enjoy their company, their laugh, their smile, and hold them in his arms and sway to the music.

It had to be the ship's air. Or maybe his sister's sappy honeymoon mood was contagious. Even if Theresa wasn't on the ship. Whatever the reason, he couldn't remember feeling this content with just being than he was right now. Taking his time to cross the lounge and rejoin Ginnie, he considered what to do next. Should he invite her to go dancing? Could he coax her into singing a duet with him? Maybe he could sneak in a stroll on deck before the kid's movie night was over.

"Did we mention that tonight's singers are being entered into a random drawing for a dinner at the specialty steakhouse?" the staffer who had been trying to coax passengers to participate announced, waving a certificate in the air.

Nick wasn't positive, but he thought he saw a sudden spark of interest in Ginnie's eyes as he moved closer.

"You were great." Her smile beamed and his heart swelled at the sight.

"Thanks. I'm a fan of old crooners, but they didn't have a whole lot of Frank Sinatra tunes on the list of choices."

"We were raised on Frank Sinatra, Dean Martin, Mario

Lanza, Lou Monte…"

Nick couldn't help but laugh. "'Dominick the Donkey'."

"Yes. You know the song?"

"It's one of my mother's favorite Christmas songs from her youth. It plays every year, and often."

"I knew our mothers would get along if they met. My mom was good friends with the son of one of the composers of that song."

"You're kidding?"

"Nope. Mom met him several times. Ray Allen. Wonderful musician and excellent entertainer."

"Wow. You tell my mother that and she'll love you and your mother for all eternity." That gave him a thought. "What are the odds that they have 'Dominick the Donkey' on karaoke?"

"Doubtful," Ginnie laughed softly.

"You're probably right." Glancing over her shoulder, he considered his next words. "Do you like steak?"

"Card carrying carnivore."

Which explained the sparkle in her eyes at the mention of a steakhouse prize. "So, are we going to look at the duets?"

Tipping her head back, she closed her eyes and shook her head. "I could just make a reservation."

"You could," he agreed. Then he turned his attention to a couple on the stage—the first note reached his ear and he winced at the sour sound. "Or we could get up there and show those two how it's done and maybe get a free dinner."

"What if I sound like nails on a chalkboard?"

"Do you?"

She shrugged. "Not that bad, but not that good either."

"I'll carry you."

Her brows rose high on her forehead and her eyes widened.

"I mean the singing."

"I know what you mean." She sighed. "Why do you want to do this anyhow?"

His turn to shrug. "I think it will be fun."

"Fun?" She actually chuckled. "I don't know about you."

"Come on. What happens at sea stays at sea."

"Who told you that?" Her brows crumpled together.

"No one. Just makes sense." He slipped his hands into his pockets. "I promise it won't be that bad."

"I can't believe I'm going to say this."

He waited as she blew out a sigh and straightened her spine and lifted her chin. She was going to say yes.

"Let's get this over with before I change my mind."

Picking out an acceptable song seemed to take longer than writing the Declaration of Independence. Most of the typical duets fell under the category of romantic and no matter how much he liked Ginnie—really liked her—singing any of those songs spelled awkward with a capital A. Just the title of 'Leather and Lace' had Ginnie blushing. Nope. This might have been the worst idea he'd ever had. Then he spotted it. Especially since technically the original song was not a duet. "This one." He tapped his finger on the sheet and in front of the staff member and bit back a laugh when Ginnie's eyes bugged out of her head.

"You're kidding?"

"Would you rather sing, 'Leather and Lace'?"

Furiously shaking her head, she waved her hands at him. "No, this song is perfect."

"Did you try calling her again?" Antoinette Ummarino had been frantic ever since she'd heard on the news that a severe storm had forced a major cruise ship to pull out to sea, leaving hundreds of passengers stranded in port.

"Mama, I'm sure she's fine or someone would have told us." Mina had been telling her mother this all day and most of the night and it wasn't doing a lick of good. Even having her sister Jo chime in wasn't helping.

"The news said the ship was allowing all passengers to have cell phone connections and refunding fees to those who had paid for a communication plan. Ginnie wouldn't waste money on it, but her phone has to be working."

Obviously, having her phone go repeatedly to voice mail was not a comfort to anyone, but Mina wasn't going to point that out to her mother.

"Hey," Jo looked up from her ringing phone, "it's Ginnie."

"Ginnie?" Her mother's face brightened as she scurried across the kitchen to stand beside her youngest daughter.

Mina crossed the kitchen even faster than her mother as the phone continued to ring. "What are you waiting for? Answer it!" *Baby sisters.*

"Hello," Jo practically shouted into the phone.

"Why are you yelling?" Mina sighed. "This isn't a couple of tin cans and string."

Jo's brows buckled together. "I can't hear very well. There's lots of clamoring."

"Clamoring?" her mother sank into the kitchen chair beside her youngest daughter. "What are you talking about? Give me that." Antoinette Ummarino yanked the phone out of her daughter's hand. "Ginnie, baby."

"Mama," Jo whined. "You know she hates it when you call her that."

The truth was, all three of them hated being called baby, but they loved their mother enough to ignore it, most of the time.

"Ginnie?" Her mother appeared perplexed.

"What is it?" Mina leaned closer to the phone. "What did she say?"

"Sam is so skinny?"

"What?"

"Something about muskrats? I can't tell. The music is too loud."

"Music?" Now both sisters were on their feet.

Reaching over her mother's shoulder, Mina punched the button for speakerphone and she realized what Jo had meant about clamoring. There was the sound of chatter and clinking glasses in the background, overshadowed by music and singing.

Her mother was right about one thing, the song was "Muskrat Love," an old hit by Captain and Tennille. "Is that Ginnie singing?"

"You're kidding?" Jo leaned in closer, squinting as if that would help her hear better.

"That's my baby's voice. So pretty. Though she never believes me." Mama smiled, listening to her daughter.

Mina, on the other hand, had a lot of questions. Starting with why in the world would Ginnie call them with no explanation to share her singing, and more importantly, who the heck was the guy singing? What a voice. And what ludicrous lyrics. She knew the seventies was a crazy time of disco balls and platform shoes, but how the heck a song about two muskrats dancing could become a billboard hit was beyond Mina's comprehension. So why the heck had her sister called her?

"Good grief," Jo exclaimed.

"What?" Mina forgot about the phone and stared up at her kid sister. "What's wrong?"

Only the shaking of Jo's shoulders with laughter put Mina at ease. "Don't you see?"

"See what?" Mama asked.

"Our practical and careful sister has just butt dialed us."

CHAPTER NINE

Who knew? Almost stumbling off the stage with laughter, it was a miracle that Ginnie managed to keep her composure on the stage. When Nick started wrinkling his nose and pursing his lips to make chirpy noises, she almost lost it. What she'd thought was the dumbest idea she'd ever heard of had turned into sheer fun.

Even the audience got a kick out of it—and to her surprise, she could actually hear people singing along as they swayed and smiled in their seats. But the real audience approval came when the lyrics sang of two muskrats whirling and twirling, and Nick took hold of her hand and spun her around in place. For a split second, she thought he was going to dip her, but then they would have missed the next line of the song. Apparently so did the audience as folks began whistling and cheering. Sure enough, at the last note, Nick did just that. He twirled her into the fold of his arms and dipped her, then quickly pulled her upright and began making the squeaky noises again.

The audience loved it, and she had to admit, she did too. When the heck was the last time any man had her laughing so hard? Especially when she was totally out of her comfort zone.

"That was great. You have a lovely voice."

"How could you tell? The audience was singing louder than we were."

"I know. The song seemed to bring back memories for lots of people."

"It must have been way more popular in its day than I would have guessed." Plopping in their seats, she tipped her head at him. "Even you seemed to know all the lyrics without reading the monitor."

He shrugged. "Growing up, when Captain and Tennille came on the radio, my mom always raised the volume. I'm afraid I know every word to 'Love Will Keep Us Together' and 'Shop Around' too."

She shook her head. "No."

"No, what?" His brows buckled at her.

"We are not doing a Captain and Tennille encore."

"No worries." Nick chuckled, patting his chest, and glanced at his watch. "I have to get the kids anyhow. That movie is almost over."

Forcing a smile, she bobbed her head. She'd actually forgotten about the children, which just made her feel worse about wishing that the evening didn't have to stop. Even if it had meant getting up there and singing another song. "Of course. I guess I lost track of time."

Nodding, he glanced over her shoulder at the stage and then sighed. "Maybe we can do this again?"

Over her inhibitions when it came to singing in public or out right making a fool of herself, without hesitating, she nodded. "Could be fun. Did Captain and Tennille do any other animal songs?"

Laughing hard, Nick kicked his head back. "I don't think so." He pushed to his feet and waited for her to do the same. "We might as well walk together as far as we can, unless you're up to wrangling four kids for a little longer?"

"Best offer I've had all night."

His head tilted to one side. "You are either an amazing person…" Then with a shrug and an impish grin, he waved for her to go first. "Or you've set your bar too low."

Without thinking, her hand swung around and slapped him lightly on the forearm.

"Okay. I may have to add feisty to amazing."

"You may have to remember I grew up with lots of male cousins, and I can take every last one of them if I had to."

"Duly noted." He bit back a smile and Ginnie found her toes tingling at the sight.

In the hall, only a few feet away from the crowded and noisy lounge, her phone rang. So unexpected, the sound not only startled her, for a few seconds it confounded her as well. All at once she remembered that she'd slid her phone into her pocket, waiting for the service to work so she could call home.

Sliding it out of her pocket, she took a quick glance at the screen and seeing her sister Mina's name, quickly tapped speaker phone. "Hello."

"You were great."

Frowning, she stared down at her cell. "What?"

"I mean, you're no Lady Gaga, but that sounded like fun."

Now Ginnie was totally confused. She actually looked over her shoulder, down the hall to see if her sisters were pranking her and had actually come on the cruise.

"You still there?" Jo's voice came through the line. "Who's the guy that sounds like he could melt ice on a freezing day?"

Ginnie's head snapped around to see Nick's eyes wide with surprise.

"Ginnie?" this time the voice was her mother's.

For land's sake, what was going on? "I'm here."

"Giovanna. Your sister is right. It's nice to hear you sing and who is the man who sings with the voice of a true Italian?"

On a sigh, Ginnie rolled her eyes at her mother's words. "Mama. Not everyone who can sing well is Italian."

His lower lip pursed over his upper lip, Nick bobbed his head, then muttered softly, "You like how I sing?"

"Is that the voice that can melt butter?" Her mother could hear a pin drop three rooms away.

"Wait a minute. Will somebody tell me what's going on? How do you know Nick can sing?"

"Ginnie, you butt dialed us. We heard almost the whole performance." Mina's voice dripped with amusement. "And nice to meet you, Nick. Kudos on talking my practical sister into singing on stage."

"Nice to meet you too, and I agree, she was great."

In the background, Ginnie could hear her mother's voice disappearing as she yelled to her husband, "Vito, your daughter found a man, just like her sisters."

Now would be a good time for the ship to hit an iceberg. She didn't dare look at Nick, yet she could almost hear his smile.

"I'm guessing you're not one of the passengers left in port?" Mina asked, probably aware that their mother had just embarrassed the dickens out of Ginnie.

"We're not, but it was a bit rocky there for a while."

"You keep us posted." Mina's tone shifted from humor to serious.

"And call us if you sing again," Jo teased.

"Right. Will do. I have to go now. It's time to pick up the kids."

"Kids?" both her sister echoed and Ginnie grinned.

"Gotta go. Bye." Hitting end call, this time she hung on to the phone, careful not to touch anything that would reconnect them. She could imagine her sisters' confusion and ensuing conversation. Ginnie loved getting the better of those two. She just wished that Nick hadn't heard most of the conversation. Of course, no one ever died from a little embarrassment. Hopefully.

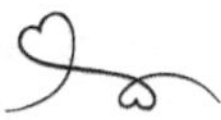

For as long as he could remember, he'd known that he could carry a tune. Heaven knew his mother and sister had told him so often enough.

One day his physics teacher heard him singing to himself at his locker and the next thing Nick knew, the guy was leaning in and nodding his head. "Try out for the school play."

His head whipped up and he wondered how many ways could he politely say no chance in hell. He wound up playing Danny in *Grease*. It had taught him several things, mostly not to be embarrassed to sing in front of people because he really did have a better than average voice. Even knowing that, hearing Ginnie and her sisters say the same thing, made him want to strut like the proverbial peacock.

That Ginnie was willing to tag along to get the kids rather than stay and play with the adults had him ready to crow. Had he ever been this happy with a woman's company? Had he ever spent this much time in less than twenty-four hours with one woman and not wanted to pull his hair out of his head by the roots or duck out the back door? Nope. Ginnie was definitely special.

His entire train of thought had him wondering, could this possibly be what the silly songs and sappy movies played up as love at first sight? Ridiculous.

"Care to share?" Strolling down the hall at his side, Ginnie glanced sideways at him. "You're shaking your head. What's up?"

"Oh." *Think fast.* "Wondering if I can get a hold of my sister now, but even if the lines work, I should probably wait for her to call me, or for morning."

Ginnie shrugged. "Or you can call after we get the kids so they can all say hello, and if she doesn't answer, leave a message."

Now he nodded instead of shaking his head. "Good plan. I like it."

The urge to reach out and hold her hand had been startling. More than once he'd shoved his hands in his pockets and then found himself reaching for her before he caught himself and once again crammed his hands back into his pockets. Timing had been perfect. Just as they rounded the corner on deck to where the kids had been watching a movie under the stars, the credits began to roll.

"Perfect timing," Ginnie glanced at him.

He smiled. "I was thinking the same thing." As they grew closer to where he remembered the kids settling in, he realized that all four were sound asleep.

"I guess the movie wasn't very good," Ginnie chuckled softly.

"Here's hoping they sleep through the night."

"It's been a long time since I was a little kid, but I'm going to guess, all this playing and hanging out in the sun is like a day at the beach, leaves you worn out and dead to the world."

"Looks like it." Nick leaned over the boys. "Time to go home."

Ginnie walked over to the girls, tapping the eldest on the shoulder. The three older ones were readily awake but the youngest at six seemed less than happy to be drawn out of her slumber. Ginnie had the little one up and on her shoulder before Nick could step in.

"I can take her."

Little Monica had already settled into Ginnie's shoulder and fallen fast asleep again. Ginnie shook her head. "I've got her."

At the elevator, he had to ask again. And when they exited the elevator, once again he had to make sure the little girl wasn't too heavy for her. Experience had taught him that eventually it was easier to put Monica on his shoulders than carry her around like the infant she no longer was. Come to think of it, his arms seemed to tire way faster than his sister's ever had when the girls were babies.

At the suite door, Nick hurried ahead to open it before Ginnie came up. Inside, his mother looked up from the sofa and her book. When her gaze fell on Ginnie carrying Monica, she smiled wider than he'd seen in a long time.

"Everyone straight to bed and put on your pajamas," his mom instructed. "Then brush your teeth and wash your hands."

"You heard your grandmother," Nick repeated, then turned to Ginnie and tapped Monica on the shoulder. "Sweetie, it's time for bed."

The kid snuggled deeper into Ginnie's shoulder and Ginnie shook her head at him. "I'll help her into her pajamas. If she doesn't wake up, we'll just leave her in bed."

"Shouldn't she go to the bathroom?" Nick thought going potty before bed was mandatory for little kids.

"If she doesn't wake up, then no." Ginnie shrugged, pulling the little one's shoes off, then her shorts and shirt. "Where's her pajamas?"

Rachel came running over with her sister's PJs. "Here you go."

Another few minutes and all the kids were brushed, washed, changed, and tucked into bed. Nick's mom had ordered room service so she was content to remain on the sofa with her leg propped up and the dish of chocolate-covered strawberries in front of her.

"Don't look at me like that." Holding a strawberry to her mouth, his mom grinned at him. "Strawberries are good for you."

"Chocolate too." Ginnie reached for one of the strawberries.

"Have more if you like. They bring us a fresh dish daily."

Ginnie shook her head. "One is plenty, thank you."

"Suit yourself." His mother opened her paperback book and didn't bother looking up. "Go have fun. I'll be here if the kids need anything."

"We've been gone long enough."

Now his mom looked up and shook her head. "Youth really is wasted on the young. Just go. You'll figure it out."

Ginnie turned to face him. "I think you've been evicted."

"Sounds like it." He swiveled around to face his mother. "Mom. You really—"

Her hand shot up, but her head remained in the book. "Go."

Spinning back to face Ginnie, if he'd learned one thing in his life, he knew there was no point in arguing with his mother. "Looks like we're out of here."

"Guess so."

He sure hoped that smile on Ginnie's face was sincere, because right now he couldn't think of anything he wanted to do more than spend time with Ginnie Ummarino.

CHAPTER TEN

If she could have, Ginnie would have gone over and kissed Nick's mother. Neither the idea of going back to her cabin to watch a movie or some shipboard updates, nor sitting alone in a lounge pretending to enjoy the piano player or adult games, held any appeal. Even though climbing into bed early and getting some much-needed rest would probably have been a good idea, spending more time with Nick sounded even better.

Pulling the door shut behind him, Nick pushed to double-check it had latched and then turned to face her. "So, where do you suggest we find something fun to make my mother happy?"

Somehow, she wished Nick hadn't phrased their time together quite that way, but it was the truth after all. "That depends on what you like to do." Flipping her wrist, she glanced at the time. "There's usually music in several of the lounges."

He smiled. "I like music."

"There's also a few games."

"Games?"

"One of my favorites is the music trivia, but I think that's earlier in the evening."

"Trivia buff?" He raised his eyebrows at her.

"Well, yes, but this is a little different. Every night is a different artist or era. Like it could be Elvis songs, or it could be movie themes, or hits of a particular decade."

"That does sound fun."

Standing at the elevator, she pulled out the daily planner she kept folded in her neck holder with her keycard. "Yep. That was an hour ago."

"Maybe tomorrow?"

"Maybe." She ignored the tingles running down her back at the thought of another day with Nick. Especially since this time it was his idea and not his mother's.

"What else is on that list?" The doors to the elevator opened and they stepped inside. "Are we going up or down?"

"Most of the activities seem to be down. We could get out on deck six and then cross the ship, see what strikes our fancy."

"Oh." He smiled. "An adventure. I like that."

No one would describe Ginnie as the adventurous one. That would have been Jo. Maybe even Mina on occasion, but she liked the idea that someone thought of her as adventurous. Or perhaps it was that Nick thought of her that way.

They'd only made it a short way down the ship when they came to the casino. Nick didn't say anything but she could tell he was eyeing the different stations with interest as they walked.

"Do you play?" she ventured.

His head turned away from the tables to his left and his gaze settled on hers. "Not really. What about you?"

She almost laughed out loud. "Not hardly. I mean, my grandmother taught us all how to play cards, poker in particular. She loved poker. But my sister Mina is the one with a sixth sense when it comes to games of chance. Or at least, she was when we took our first cruise."

"So you've never played the slot machines anywhere?"

She shook her head.

"What about roulette?"

"Only if casino night at my Catholic high school counts."

"I thought the Catholics had the corner on Bingo."

"That too. But casino night was the annual fundraiser. It always brought in the big bucks. One year we got a brand spanking new chemistry lab. Even kids who didn't like science loved that lab."

"Is there a story there?"

"Not mine. Though it was awfully entertaining when George Carlyle and Tommy Benson almost blew the place up. If Sister Margaret hadn't walked in when she did and threw their test tubes out the window, the little explosion that burned half the lawn probably would have blown out all the windows."

"I see." His gaze lingered a moment at one of the tables. "Want to stop?"

"That guy seems to be doing well." Nick lifted his chin, pointing at a man shaking dice in his hands.

Though she'd never played, or even seen it played anywhere but in a back alley in an old movie, she thought she recognized that table. "Craps?"

He nodded and the guy let the dice roll. From the way the folks standing around the table cheered, she suspected that it was a good thing.

"Let's stay and watch."

"You don't mind?"

She shook her head. If it was with Nick, she'd gladly stand around and watch paint dry. "Can you explain what's happening?"

His head bobbed. "Sure."

They inched closer to the table and slid in between two people, forcing her and Nick to stand so close that she could feel his arm brush against hers. She had to resist the urge to lean in even closer.

"Now, if he throws a seven or an eleven, he'll win. If the dice lands on two, three, or twelve, that's not good."

As if the dice were following Nick's explanation, the two numbers rolled and stopped at eleven and the entire table gave a collective sigh.

"Now what?"

"He can't do anything now. He has to pass his turn."

"Okay. Got it." She watched the next woman toss the dice. People were moving chips around. Every few tosses some folks cheered and others groaned. For the life of her, Ginnie could not figure out how the heck this game worked. Obviously, seven or eleven were good and two, three, and twelve weren't, but everything in between was a mystery to her.

"Want to give it a try?"

It took her a second to realize that Nick was talking to her. Not that he'd be talking to anyone else, but if anything, she would have thought he would want a chance to play. "What about you? Don't you want to play?"

"I'm not very lucky at games of chance. I guarantee you if I take the dice, I'll get snake eyes."

Even she knew that was the dreaded two. "You can't be that bad. Chance means chance on either side of the fence."

He shook his head. "Okay, but you'll see."

Taking the dice in his hand, he did a quick shake, no blowing or prayer or calling on lady luck. As a matter of fact, now that she thought about it, none of the players had been as melodramatic about shooting dice as the movies. Debating whether or not she should cross her fingers, or maybe cross herself, she did neither and kept her gaze on the dice. One landed, then the other, they rolled, tilted, and stopped. Snake eyes. "And there you go. No luck tonight."

"I see what you mean."

If Nick could predict winning lottery numbers as easily as he could predict losing at craps, he'd be a very wealthy man by now. "I really enjoy the game, but don't have the touch."

"I'll be honest. I haven't a clue what's going on, but it is fun to watch. There's an odd energy around the table."

"I'll agree about the energy, not sure odd is the right word for it, but it's definitely there. You should give it a try. Something new for you."

"I'd probably throw snake eyes just like you."

"Or maybe not understanding what you're doing will bring you beginner's luck. Feed off the energy."

"I don't know."

"My mother did say find something fun to do. This can be fun…" He had no idea why he was pushing so hard for her to play, but the way she seemed to be eyeing everyone at the table, he thought he caught a glimmer of interest, much like a kid on the school yard who wants to be in on the game.

"I suppose for your mother." Her eyes sparkled and her shoulders did a little enthusiastic pop. He'd been right, she had been itching to try.

Once the current player tossed a seven and crapped out, the dice came to Ginnie.

Picking up the dice in one hand, she lifted her other hand and Nick quickly touched her forearm. "Sorry, only one hand and always keep it over the table."

Her brows buckled in what he thought might be confusion.

"I'll explain later."

Nodding, she shook the dice, whispered something to herself that no one, not even he could hear. Closing her eyes, she threw the dice onto the table. Not till a handful of people to her left cheered did she open them and see the eleven. "Oh, my."

"There you go," he waved an arm at the dice on the table. "Beginner's luck."

She nodded. After the dealer paid out the winning bets, he pushed the dice back at her with a long stick that resembled a shepherd's crook. Once again she held the dice over the table and muttered something only she knew. Just as before, she closed her eyes and let the dice roll across the table. Seven. Another instant winner. The same folks to the left who had bet with her, cheered loudly.

Again, her brows buckled and she leaned into him. "How come the guy before me lost with a seven and I won?"

"I'll explain later. Keep rolling."

Doing as instructed, she threw the dice again, rolling an eight.

"Did I win?" she asked softly.

"You didn't lose. You can hedge your bets by giving the gentleman another number. Do you want to?"

"Sure."

"What number?"

Her eyebrows shot up on her forehead and he was almost tempted to see if he'd grown horns. "Four, five, six, nine or ten."

"Six."

"Tell him, not me."

"Right." Letting the croupier know, she threw the same dice again. The woman's luck was holding. Another six.

When the dealer paid out again, Ginnie's eyes lit up and her feet did a little jig. The pile of chips in her tray was growing. With every toss and success, the crowd around the table grew. With luck like this, she should play the lottery.

"I don't want to bet anymore." Ginnie took a short step in retreat and spoke so only he could hear. "This can go on forever. Aren't we supposed to quit while we're ahead?"

"Not in craps. You don't have to keep betting so much, when you hit your eight or crap out, then you can stop."

"All I need is an eight or snake eyes."

"No. Eight or Seven."

"Seven loses."

He nodded.

"Like the guy before me?"

"Sort of, yes."

"This is confusing."

Now that she mentioned it, it had taken him a long time to learn all the rules about what you throw and when you throw. "A little, but keep shooting or we may have a revolt on our hands."

One more throw and she hit the eight. The dealer paid out, and as she collected her chips. As she walked away from the table, the folks who had been winning by betting alongside her gave her a brief round of applause.

"What do you want to play now?"

"Nothing. I want to take my money and get out of here while I'm ahead. I've heard too many stories of people winning at gambling and then losing it all right away."

At the cashier's window, she handed over her chips and her eyes grew wider and wider as the cashier counted out over five hundred dollars. All the money in hand, she spun around and grinning, pointed a finger at him. "Wow. I still don't quite understand how I did this, but thank you. I owe you the biggest steak dinner you ever had."

"You don't owe me anything, but if that's an invitation, I accept."

"Consider yourself invited."

"Then consider your invitation accepted." He may not have won shooting craps for himself, but if he had still more excuses to spend time with Ginnie, then tonight he was definitely a winner too.

CHAPTER ELEVEN

The kids falling asleep early had nothing on Ginnie. By the time she'd collected her winnings at the casino, she'd begun yawning. Just a smidge at first, but once they'd reached the music lounge, she was yawning more than breathing. She had begrudgingly agreed that the day had been long and an early night in bed would be the ticket. Which meant leaving Nick at the elevator. Had she ever felt so connected to someone, besides her sisters?

She'd asked herself that question all night and dreamt about it too. At least Nick had invited her to join them for breakfast if she was up to wrangling the kids again. With sincere delight, she'd accepted in a heartbeat. Now she found herself scrambling to dress and meet them at the suite at the designated time.

The entire ride up the elevator and the walk down the hallway to the suite, her heart was practically dancing the two step with every excited beat. Not since high school could she remember looking so forward to spending time with the opposite sex, but here she was, anticipation for the day growing with every step. She actually had to take a second and suck in a deep calming breath before knocking on the door.

Within seconds the door flung open. Jake, the older boy, hollered *we're almost ready* as he turned on his heel and ran back inside.

"Come on in." Nick's mom waved from her spot on the sofa. The woman was already dressed in tan capris with a black sleeveless, neatly pressed shirt. If not for the wrapped foot perched up on the stack of pillows, no one would know she was even slightly inconvenienced on this trip.

"We decided to order breakfast in." Nick came hurrying out from his room, tucking his shirt into his waistband. "Thought it might be less chaotic."

"I'm setting the table." Flashing a grin that exposed two missing front teeth and her stuffed bunny tucked snuggly under one arm, Monica stood proudly in front of Ginnie, holding a glass in each hand.

"Be careful setting those on the table." Mrs. Maroney smiled at the child.

Ginnie's gaze lifted to the expanse of patio doors across the far wall. On the deck that was larger than her entire backyard, she spotted the patio table already decorated with a vase of flowers and what looked like the coveted chocolate covered strawberries.

Moving further inside to see what she could help with, a rap on the door sounded behind her. With a quick spin around, she opened the door. On the other side, the steward waited ready to push the loaded cart into the suite.

"Where shall I put this?" the young man asked.

Nick appeared at the man's side, pointing to the balcony. "Outside would be great."

With a nod, the man wheeled the cart forward, then, one by one, lifted the metal covered dishes and placed them on the large table. "If you need anything else, let me know."

After a few nods, and thank yous, and small people moving about, everyone was finally seated at the table, including Nick's mother, despite her son's objections.

"There's plenty of everything so eat up." Nick slathered butter and syrup on the pancakes for Monica and Rachel, while his mother looked on smiling, and the boys insisted they didn't need anyone's help.

"What are the plans for today?" Ginnie cut into a slice of melon. It amazed her that Nick had not only paid attention to the food she'd been ordering, but had ordered food especially for her.

"What do you say, kids? Another day at the club?" Nick bit into his English muffin with honey.

"Yeah!" the boys cheered.

The girls didn't look as convinced about the idea.

"What do you think?" Ginnie asked the two girls.

"Can we stay with you?" Monica said.

What the children did with their day was not Ginnie's decision to make. Heck, she'd only been invited to breakfast. For all she knew, Nick intended to spend his day napping when Phoebe napped, or sunbathing, or finding some guys to play poker with. The possibilities on the ship were endless.

"Can we?" Rachel repeated.

Ginnie glanced in Nick's direction, their gazes met, and she could read his eyes like the proverbial book. He wanted her to decide. She shook her head. "That's up to Uncle Nick."

This time he tipped his head slightly and cocked his brows at her. Okay. So, was that an invitation?

All she could do was smile and shrug.

Holding her gaze, he straightened his head, gave a slight bob of his chin, and smiled.

How she knew he was asking confirmation she had no idea. She felt like a poodle and a German Shepherd communicating in a dog park. Biting back the urge to laugh at the ridiculous conversation they'd just held, she nodded and grinned.

"Guess we're hanging out together today." Nick ruffled the hair on the top of the little one's head.

"Wait," the bigger boy chimed in. "What are you going to do?"

"Yeah," the younger brother, who Ginnie noticed tended to follow his older brother's lead, looked to Nick.

"I suppose we could play miniature golf?"

All four kids stared silently at him.

"Or how about cards or puzzles in the game room?"

Still no reaction.

"They have one heck of a water park. We could spend the day at the pool?"

Like the starting shot at a track race, all the kids bounced up from their seats and began running in different directions.

"Hey. Where's everyone going?" Nick asked.

"To put on my bathing suit," Jake answered from his bedroom doorway, and all the others nodded.

Nick shook his head. "Not till you finish breakfast."

With less spring in their step, the four marched back to their seats and poked at breakfast.

"You know," his mom smiled at the children, "the faster you finish eating, the sooner you can hit the pool."

Once again, enthusiasm reigned. Ginnie had never seen anyone demolish their breakfast as fast as these kids. "I should probably head back to my cabin and change."

"Oh, yeah." Nick chuckled. "Me too." He pushed away from the table. "Meet you back here in…?"

"Ten minutes," she finished, then hurried out the door and practically ran down the hall. She didn't even like swimming, but right now she couldn't think of anything more fun to do than swim in a crowded pool on a massive ship with Nick and five children. Her mother would be laughing herself silly if she could see Ginnie now.

Much to Nick's surprise, instead of being overwhelmed by his sister's absence and his mother's injured leg, he was thrilled to have an excuse to spend more time with Ginnie. There was nothing about his plans for this vacation that included meeting women. Or a woman. This was a trip for Uncle Nick, and while he was at it, a little quality time with his mother. Instead, his mind was wandering to how much he was going to hate to have this cruise end.

Working their way to the pool, they'd run into another couple with a child Phoebe's age on their way to the toddler care. The two toddlers had obviously made friends, so at the last minute he and Ginnie decided to leave Phoebe at the ship's babysitting with her little friend.

Now, on deck, rummaging through a beach bag big enough to store the state of Rhode Island, Ginnie looked up at Nick. "Who has the sunscreen? I thought I tossed it in here."

"I have it." The oldest girl raised her hand, the fingers gripping the large tube of sunscreen. "Monica and I burn easily if we don't use the good stuff."

Rachel never ceased to surprise him. Sometimes she was such a kid, getting into mischief like any other child. Other times, it seemed she was nine going on forty.

"It will only wash off when we get in the pool." Jake frowned at his new sister.

"Not the good stuff." Rachel plopped one hand on her hip and used a patriarchal tone that reminded Nick so much of his sister, he had to fight not to laugh.

"Everyone should use sunscreen all the time." Ginnie slathered the lotion onto Jeff's back and one by one made sure each child had extra coverage behind their necks and ears and on the tops of their feet.

"I would never have thought to do that."

Slathering lotion on her own feet, she glanced up at him. "You must never have come home with lobster feet."

Again, he bit back a laugh. "Can't say that I ever have."

When Ginnie straightened and pulled her cover-up over her head and tossed it aside, he almost swallowed his tongue. A very modest one piece suit reminiscent of movies from the fifties that covered everything it possibly could, was nothing that should have had his pulse racing, but on her curves it was nonetheless.

"Could you please put this on my back?" She stood, arm stretched, holding the tube of sunscreen.

For the life of him, he couldn't get his mouth to move. His tongue felt like it was stuck in a vat of peanut butter.

"Nick?"

"Sorry." One word was all he could manage. Taking hold of the lotion, he sucked in a deep breath, rubbed it between his hands so it wouldn't be too cold, and began gently spreading it across her back and shoulders. When his fingers slid under the strap of the swimsuit to ensure she didn't burn if the straps moved, his heart rate stuttered. He was definitely a guy, and men reacted to beauty, they were just wired that way, but this feeling that he could simply stand here and apply lotion to her back for the next ten or twenty years was shockingly new.

"Are we going in the water now?" Monica stood at Nick's side.

"Yes," he managed to get out. "Yes, we are." Closing the lid on the lotion, he handed it back to her.

"Want me to put some on your back?"

His head snapped from side to side a little more vehemently than it should have, but the last thing he needed right now was her fingertips on any part of him. "No, thanks. I, uh, don't burn easily."

"You sure?" Her brows crinkled into an unhappy V. "Skin cancer is no fun."

He continued to shake his head. "You're right, of course, but I'm fine."

"If you insist." She slid the tube into the massive beach bag and turned to the children. "Last one in is a rotten egg."

Before he had time to process, Ginnie had her arms over her head and had dived into the massive pool and popped up on the other side with the grace of Esther Williams and the skill of Katie Ledecky.

A moment later all four kids had jumped in and were chasing after her. It didn't hurt any that, to his surprise, the pool wasn't nearly as crowded as he'd seen it on other days.

Just as he'd jumped in after everyone, one of the guys responsible for outdoor fun blew his whistle and got everyone's attention. "Who's ready for a race?"

Of course every kid in the pool shouted their interest.

"All right. We're going to line up at the opposite end of the pool, just like the Olympics," he said as several littler ones looked left and right in an effort to follow the staff member's instructions. "But first you'll have to do a height check with the other member of the entertainment staff."

One by one all the kids lined up, several were deemed too short, but all four of Nick's family made the cut. He was thankful that Phoebe was at the toddler program or he'd be too distracted to follow the races.

The first effort was pretty entertaining. Using kickboards, the kids kicked and splashed and bumped into each other until all made it across the pool to the applause and cheers of friends, family, and even strangers.

"All right. Now we want kids and parents," the same guy announced into the mic.

Eyes wide, Ginnie looked to Nick, a hint of panic visible. He couldn't blame her. What were they getting into?

CHAPTER TWELVE

A handful of kids stood shivering at the crew staff's side with a parent behind them, a couple of kids had one parent with a hand on each kid's shoulder, but Nick's four stood looking over their shoulders at him.

"Come on, Uncle Nick," Jeff waved him over.

"Yeah, Ginnie," Rachel shouted, making her smile that she was included in whatever mess they were about to get into.

On a sigh, Nick nodded at her and together they took their places behind two children.

"All right. Since there's plenty of room in the pool today, we're going to shift this up. We're doing raft races, kids against adults."

Of course the kids erupted in another round of cheers, jumping up and down, and pretty much every adult groaned, with the exception of one or two dads who seemed to have a healthy competitive streak.

"Each child will have a tanning float. The idea is to get to the end of the pool first. Each family will go one at a time. The rest will cheer them on, and after every family has had a turn, we'll tally the kids and adult times for the winner."

Some of the kids frowned, a few cheered, and Ginnie waited for the other shoe to drop. She'd been on these cruises and watched these games enough to know there was always more to the story.

"There's one little catch," the staffer announced.

Ginnie leaned into Nick. "I knew it."

"You kids will notice the yellow floats. Those are for you. Each child gets their own float. You have to lay on your stomach and paddle forward till you reach the other side."

Every kid nodded.

"Adults…"

"Here it comes," Ginnie muttered.

"The blue wider floats are for you, but we ran out of time to fully inflate them, so you'll have to finish blowing them up before you can get in the pool."

One wife laughed, informing her husband since he was full of hot air, he could blow it up.

"I suppose it's only fair to give us a handicap," Nick agreed.

"And there's one other thing," the crew staff continued.

"Get ready, here it comes." Ginnie sighed.

Nick glanced in her direction. "Blowing up our own floats isn't enough?"

"We're a little short on blue floats so parents, you'll have to share."

"Share?" several voices spoke up.

"That's right. Just like your kids, you'll lay on your stomach. This is all about showing your kids teamwork. Each spouse will have one arm around the other so you'll only have one arm to paddle with."

Agreeing to do this may not have been Ginnie's smartest move. A handful of parents pointed out they didn't have partners present and the crew gave them permission to pick another friend or family member as long as it wouldn't lead to divorce. Somehow, most folks observing found that more humorous than Ginnie had.

"On your mark, get set, go."

At the word go, all the kids jumped into the pool with their floats and proceeded to climb on, some at the first try, others took a little longer. The first batch of kids were halfway across when their parents joined them. Something told Ginnie this wasn't the family's first effort because the husband and wife seemed to know exactly what they were doing with only a couple of bouts of spinning in the wrong direction before arriving across the pool a few strokes behind their kids.

They were up next. Ginnie turned to Nick. "Anything I can do to help?"

"I wish."

The man did his *ready, set, go,* and all of Nick's family jumped into the pool. The girls were able to mount their floats sooner than the boys, but the boys weren't far behind. On deck, Nick looked like a puffer fish, blowing into the float with everything he had. With four kids in the pool, bumping into each other happened more than with just two, but they were halfway across when Nick plugged the float. "This is good enough. Ready?"

Somehow, she doubted she'd ever be ready to be up close and personal with Nick Maroney.

Part of Nick wished that Ginnie would chicken out. The idea of being plastered next to her in a silly race was not the reason he'd want to have his arms around her for the very first time.

"As ready as I'll ever be." Ginnie's smile struck him as being awfully shaky, but when her shoulders straightened and she reached for the float, he knew she was in competition mode. Hanging onto the float with one hand, she hopped into the pool and held the float steady. "You first."

Why not? Grabbing onto the corner, he studied this for a second and decided climbing on and then rolling over made the most sense. One leg over the top, he sat first, then laid out. Not bad. Except he was in the middle of the float. "Let me shift left, then you climb on."

Ginnie nodded.

Holding on to the top corners, he shifted his hips and the whole float flipped over, dumping him into the water. Popping up from underwater, he wiped his face and spotted Ginnie spitting laughter at him.

"Maybe I should get on first."

"Sure." Obviously, he'd botched it.

With the grace he'd expect of her, she slipped on and straddled the float. "Climb on first, then we'll lie down."

"Here goes nothing." Swinging his leg over, he climbed on behind her. So far, so good.

Up ahead, he could see the kids making progress. Jake had slid off and had to climb back on. Jeff had accidentally spun around and bumped into Monica, knocking both of them off their floats, and like a good big sister, Rachel had turned around to help her sister climb back on in the slightly deeper waters.

"All right." Ginnie raised her hand for a high-five slap and almost fell backward.

Quickly, Nick grabbed her arms, holding them steady until the water stopped sloshing underneath them.

Ginnie's gaze momentarily locked with his, and he swore he saw the same longing that had been building inside him. On a sigh, she tore her gaze away. "I think you should lie down first, but this time, lean forward not back."

"Can't we just paddle sitting up?" He knew better but had to suggest it.

Shaking her head, her mouth twisting to one side, Ginnie's entire face crinkled in thought. "Maybe we should both raise a leg at the same time?"

"What?" How the heck were they supposed to do that without knocking each other off the float?

"Got a better idea?"

All he could do was sigh and shake his head. "How about I lean forward and you lean back and we see what happens?"

Slowly as her head nodded, her one leg came up. They looked like a modern sculpture of chaos in motion. As her leg lifted, she leaned right.

"Don't rock the boat!" Nick shouted, holding his arms out to stabilize the float, before attempting the same maneuver. Next thing he knew, his knee collided with hers and they both went over one side into the pool—again.

Wiping the water out of his eyes, Nick looked up to see that Jake had reached the end of the pool and was climbing out, while he and Ginnie hadn't even managed to start. From deck side, the gathering of cheering adults had grown, some shouting suggestions that seemed anatomically impossible.

One more time, they tried a new strategy. Nick climbed on, slowly, and managed to lean forward, bringing his legs up onto the float and leaving him flat on his stomach.

Throwing her arms up in the air, Ginnie shouted triumphantly as if she'd been the one to climb aboard, "Okay, here goes nothing!"

Where had he heard *that* before. The plan, that he wasn't thrilled with but seemed to be the only one to hold a chance of success, was for her to climb up onto his back, move to lie forward, then slide to the side. The second she threw one leg over him and hefted herself onto his back, he asked himself, not for the first time, why was this the way they'd chosen to get up close and personal.

"All right!" Her arms shot up again and the float wobbled left then right. "Oops."

"Oops?" He lifted his head slightly to glance at her immediately regretting the move when the float dipped right.

Stretching her arms out to her sides, her bottom wriggled along his back as she tried to catch their balance.

Nick bit back a groan and let his head flop down, burying his face in the float. Thank heaven he wasn't on his back.

The float steady again, Ginnie leaned forward, barely brushing against him as she raised her legs and slid to the right.

All set to drop his left arm in the water and start paddling, he remembered he was supposed to place his other arm around her. Raising his arm and carefully curling it around her waist, he leaned slightly left and in one large wave, the two rolled over and dumped into the pool at the same moment the last of the kids climbed out, the four laughing and cheering and jumping up and down in triumph.

Standing upright and spitting out water and wiping their faces, in an unexpected moment of unity, both of them burst out laughing. At least the kids were having fun, and if he were honest with himself, so was he.

CHAPTER THIRTEEN

"Of course the kids won."

Ginnie came out of Phoebe's room as Nick explained to his mother how their morning had gone.

"It was awesome." Jake grinned at his new grandmother.

"Yeah," Rachel agreed. "Can we do it again?"

Both Nick and Ginnie groaned, then burst into laughter at the unplanned synchrony.

"I'm sure if there's another race you can." His mom grinned up at them. If she'd had any idea how embarrassing the whole attempt was, she might not have been so eager to volunteer them. "Who knows, maybe by then I'll be able to get around a bit and see for myself."

Just what she didn't need, to put on a display of anatomical awkwardness in front of Nick's mother.

"How is your foot feeling?"

"Better," Mrs. Maroney said. "I can set it down for a few minutes before it throbs. I'm sure in a couple of days I'll be able to comfortably go with you guys on at least one adventure."

Adventure. That about described the morning. Maybe.

"What's on the agenda for this afternoon?" she continued.

"There's a scavenger hunt." Nick squatted down by the coffee table where the kids had set up for lunch and handed each of the kids the sandwiches room service had delivered.

"Yeah." Jeff grinned up. "We have to go all around the ship looking for stuff. Uncle Nick says it will be fun."

Ginnie had her doubts about keeping up with not only

Nick's family but everyone else's kids running about, but if she'd learned anything coming from a large family, it was to go with the flow and say your Hail Marys while you're at it.

"Why don't you two go have a nice quiet lunch until it's time for Phoebe to wake up?"

"We've already ordered lunch." Nick lifted the cover from the burgers he'd ordered.

"You're eating hamburgers?" His mother shook her head at him. "Every food imaginable and you order a hamburger."

Nick shrugged and Ginnie was suddenly very happy she'd ordered a BLT, though she didn't know if that would be anymore interesting for his mom.

"At least go sit out on the patio." His mother waved an arm toward the sliding doors.

Their eyes met and with a short nod, they agreed to move outside for lunch. Plates in hand, Nick followed her. To her surprise, expecting him to sit across from her at the large table, he set his place down beside her. "I'll be back out with our drinks."

Her gaze lingered on his back as he walked into the suite. He paused a moment to ask his mother something, then grabbed the two bottled waters and turned around. A bottle in each hand, he held them up and smiled.

She could run through a pretty long list about now of all the things she liked about Nick. Thoughtful. Considerate. Polite. Loves his family. Good sense of humor. Winsome smile. Amazing voice. And deep eyes she could melt into if she let herself. For just a second, she considered how much she was going to miss having him around when the cruise was over, and just like that, an ache filled her chest where only moments ago her heart had been beating merrily waiting for him to join her.

Could it be that just like her sisters, she'd gone and fallen for a stranger on a ship?

"Here you go." Nick unscrewed the cap and set the bottle with the glass he'd brought on the table in front of her and shot her an even brighter smile that made her toes curl.

Yep. She'd done it. She'd fallen head over sandals in love with a man she might never see again after a few more days. Now her heart really hurt.

It took every ounce of self-control Nick had not to set her drink down and lean over and steal a kiss while he was at it. Not a ravishing *can I take you on the table top* kiss, but a sweet, sensitive press of lips to show her just how much she'd come to mean to him. And how much was that? So many things he admired about her. The way she just stepped in to help. Sacrificed her own fun for people she hardly knew. Smiled at his dumb jokes. Laughed at the same things he did. And the way her hips swayed when she walked could mesmerize a blind man. But most of all, he loved how they could talk about anything, whether for snatches of five minutes of time, or whole hours. Not that they'd had that many opportunities to chat for longer than over dinner, but he'd enjoyed every word she'd said. No matter how you sliced it, he loved being around Ginnie. Everything was just better when she was involved.

Everything was better with her. The words played around in his head. Could this be it? Was this what being in love felt like?

Wiping a smidge of mayo away from the corner of her mouth, Ginnie smiled sheepishly, her cheeks turning a lovely shade of pink and her deep brown eyes sparkling with a combination of humor and embarrassment. His heart did a kick and he could hear it shouting at him: *you're in love, you idiot.* Head over heels, hook line and sinker in love.

How was that even possible? Didn't people need time— lots of time—to know if someone was the one?

Swallowing, Ginnie tipped her head and her smile softened. "Don't like your lunch?"

"Hmm?" He shifted his attention to his untouched hamburger. "Oh, no. I was just thinking."

"About?" She leaned over and took another bite.

Even the way she ate was cute. Aw, hell. If there was such a thing as love at first sight, this was it. He was very much in love with Miss Ginnie Ummarino. Which left one question: what the heck was he going to do about it? "Dance with me?"

"I'm sorry, what?" She stared at him as if he'd sprouted a third eye, or worse, horns.

"I mean tonight. After the kids go to bed. Let's go dancing?"

Her soft smile tilted up higher. "I'd like that."

"Are we still going for the scavenger hunt?" Jake popped his head out the door.

"We are." Nick turned his wrist and glanced at his watch. "But it doesn't start till after Phoebe wakes up from her nap."

"Okay." Jake ran back inside and Nick heard Rachel call out, "If we wake Phoebe up we can go."

Like a shot, Nick was up and out of his seat. "No!"

Chuckling, Ginnie came running in behind him. "We have to wait for the right time to go and it's not now."

Three faces fell with disappointment, but Monica pulled her favorite bunny closer against her chest and frowned. Nick had his doubts she believed them, but it looked like she was going to take their advice at face value.

None of which mattered because in about ten minutes, as if she'd heard every word of conversation over the sound machine inside, Phoebe stirred.

"Do you want to get her or shall I?"

"I'll do it. You've had to change more than your share of diapers for a vacation."

"I don't mind." Ginnie really did have a marvelous smile, especial when it made her eyes light up.

"Next time."

"Oh." His mother snapped her fingers. "I almost forgot. I got a call from your sister. The weather on the island is finally clearing up. They're booked to fly out tomorrow too late to meet the ship, but at the next port they should return on board. She also said the cruise line is reimbursing all of us for the cost of the cruise *and* we also will get a free cruise."

"Wow, a two for one. Leaving so many passengers stranded must be a royal screw up." Nick wished he could get the same deal for Ginnie; after all, she'd pretty much given up her vacation to help him keep up with the kids.

Another fun thing he had to admit about this trip: Phoebe was always cute, but every time she woke up from a nap and curled into his arms, laying her head into his shoulder, he swore he could melt. He'd gotten hugs before, but never the snuggles like the one that came after naptime.

With the kids all gathered together, they headed over to the toddler camp, but Phoebe refused to let go of her uncle's neck. "Don't you want to play with your friends?" he asked.

Laying her head down on his shoulder was her only response.

"I guess that's a no."

"Do you want to come with me?" Ginnie wiggled her fingers at Phoebe and with a big grin, the toddler flung herself into Ginnie's arms. "I'm guessing that is a yes. This is a family event, she can join us."

"I should have brought the stroller."

"Nah." Ginnie shook her head. "Folks would just trip over it. No one ever looks down."

"I suppose."

"Trust me." She chuckled. "My sister Jo is always in a hurry to get somewhere and she never looks down. On our cruises she was constantly tripping over strollers and bumping into motorized scooters. Carrying Phoebe will be easier in the long run."

"Yes, ma'am." He almost saluted her.

When they reached the area for the start of the scavenger hunt, he wasn't surprised by the crowd gathered around the central lobby. The same guy who had run the float races was explaining how the photo scavenger hunt worked. They were told to take pictures according to the instructions on the list they'd been given. The first being a family photo by the queen.

"I know!" Jake grabbed his brother's hand and took off

straight ahead.

Without a word, the girls followed quickly, with Nick and Ginnie scrambling to keep up. Down the hall, across the deck, and Jake was running down the stairs, two steps at a time.

Each kid spinning and jumping onto the landing until Jake stopped in front of a photograph. "Here she is. The Queen. Mom pointed her out the first day of the cruise."

Yes, indeed. A portrait of the Queen of the Netherlands hung prominently on the wall beside Jake. The next trick was to get a selfie with all seven of them in it. As soon as they managed that, the kids were off running in search of the next clue.

Ginnie shifted Phoebe to her other hip and chuckling, looked up at Nick. "Your sister must be in great shape, because I think I've just found the perfect diet plan. Chase kids on a scavenger hunt."

"You don't need to diet."

"And you, my dear friend, would make a wonderful diplomat."

He smiled at her, but the word friend didn't sit well with him. He was going to have to do something about that. And soon.

CHAPTER FOURTEEN

Staring into her closet, Ginnie wondered what the heck should she wear. It wasn't like this was a real date…was it? No, Nick was probably just anxious for a little adult time without kids. She should not make a big deal about it. Still, she did want to look nice. Just not too nice. She didn't want to scare him off, after all.

When Ginnie left Nick's suite, all the kids except Jake had fallen asleep before the word "bedtime" had been spoken. The girls had been coloring on the floor and fell asleep right there and the younger boy fell asleep on the sofa beside Nick's mom as she read him a story. The older boy helped his brother into bed while Nick carried the girls to their beds. Ginnie had helped him get the girls out of their clothes and into their pajamas. The surprising thing was that neither girl even blinked. Who knew an afternoon of photography scavenger hunting could wear kids out so much?

Though if she were honest, crawling into bed and getting a very long night's sleep held a great deal of appeal, just nowhere near the appeal of time alone with Nick. Well, alone with a few thousand other people.

Wanting to dress up a little but still look casual, she settled for a royal blue sundress that always complimented her Mediterranean complexion, and for good luck, she put on her pearls. She'd barely stepped into her sling back sandals when a rap sounded at her door. Instantly, her heart soared. When she flung the door open, Nick stood on the other side in a neatly pressed, button-down shirt with the sleeves rolled halfway up his forearms. Damn, that man looked hot. "Hi."

"Hi." The way his eyes sparkled when she smiled only added to how handsome he looked. The shirt didn't hurt any either. "Ready to go?"

She nodded and stepping out into the hall, pulled the door shut behind her. "All set."

Halfway down the hall, he stretched his arm out and snatched her hand in his. "Do you mind?"

Shaking her head, she smiled up at him. "Not at all."

His smile widened and she gave herself permission to hope that maybe, just maybe, whatever this thing between them was, would work itself out.

The ship had several different choices for nighttime entertainment. Singers and musical groups from a one-man band to classical harpists and popular trios played all over the ship, but Nick led them to one lounge in particular. Smaller than some, it had a wall of windows that allowed for a view of the ocean. Tonight the moon cast a stream of light, shimmering on the water. At the opposite side, a small bar with limited seating was a buzz of activity. Scattered around the small parquet dance floor, several tables and chairs were already spoken for, but several more were still available. At the piano a young man played tunes that had folks tapping their toes and occasionally singing along. In between sets, canned music played overhead. All of it perfectly suited for dancing.

Seated by the piano at the front of the dance floor, Ginnie toyed with her Marvelous Mango.

"Do you always choose fruity drinks like that?" Nick asked.

"Not really. At home, I love a good glass of chianti, but on the ships, they always make fun drinks. Each cruise I find one I like and then I stick with it. Even though this doesn't taste at all like a mango, it's tasty as heck nonetheless."

"I'll try and remember that."

"You're a really good uncle."

"Thanks, I try. Especially since Chuck died. I hated seeing my sister go through hell."

"I can't even imagine." She barely knew Nick and if

anything happened to him, she already knew she'd be beyond heartbroken. The somber mood shifted as the piano player banged out one of her favorite tunes by Bill Withers and her toes started tapping to the catchy beat. "Oh, I love Bill Withers. Such an eclectic singer, but this is one of my favorite songs of his."

"Shall we?" Nick stood and extended his hand to her.

Without a word she pushed to her feet and slipping her hand in his, followed him to the dance floor. The sweet beat justified him curling her into the fold of his arms and gently swaying as they moved around the floor.

"Seems you dance as well as you sing." Ginnie lifted her gaze to meet his.

"You're making me look good."

That had her cackling out a low laugh. "My mother will be delighted to hear that all those years of dance lessons paid off."

They remained on the floor for the next couple of songs until the piano player announced he was taking a break and they returned to their seats.

"Did you really take dance lessons?"

Ginnie nodded. "Starting at age four I took everything from ballet, jazz and tap, to ballroom dancing for cotillion in junior high."

"I guess everyone does cotillion. My mother both threatened and bribed me to go."

"From what I've seen on the floor, it paid off."

He shook his head. "Nah, my grandmother taught me how to dance. My grandfather explained the fine art of leading, but it was Grams who would drag me into the living room at every family gathering and make sure I learned enough not to step on anyone's feet."

"I think I'd have liked her."

"Maybe some day you can meet her. She's eighty-nine and feisty as ever."

"Oh, I love that!" A thump behind her chair startled her, making her look over her shoulder.

"Excuse me," the man she'd noticed that first night at karaoke, apologized as he swayed toward the bar.

"Something tells me it's not the ship rocking that has him swaying with the boat." Ginnie couldn't help but wonder what the deal was with this guy. If anything could lift a person's spirits it was a cruise, and yet, not with him. She'd felt sorry for him the other night and nothing had changed.

"Guess he didn't find anyone to help mend that broken heart." Nick watched the guy slide onto a bar stool. "Too bad."

"Yeah." How come she was blessed to have stumbled into Nick and that poor man only had the drink in front of him, she didn't know, but she'd never been more thankful in her life.

Nick couldn't believe he had a legitimate reason to hold Ginnie in his arms. When the piano player took his break and they walked back to their seats, he prayed the canned music would give him a reason to take her back out on the floor.

Not even feeling sorry for the poor guy burying his sorrows at the bar could take away from how he felt being here with Ginnie. Somewhere in the last few days he'd learned that they only lived about forty-five minutes away from each other. Not quite around the corner but it beat cross country. He just hoped her acceptance of his invitation and her willingness to let him hold her hand as they'd walked to the lounge also meant she'd be open to seeing him when they got back home.

Overhead he recognized another Bill Withers tune. "Ready for another turn on the floor?"

"Absolutely."

When the man sang about "Just the two of us" Nick twirled her in place, curling her back into the fold of his arms. With her pressed up close and personal, he couldn't help himself. His steps slowed and their gazes locked. He could almost feel her heartbeat against him. There was no stopping where this was going. No controlling how he felt. Pulling her impossibly closer, he leaned forward, and quickly taking in everything reflected in her eyes, he closed the gap and let his lips press against hers.

His arms tightened around her waist, and when her fingers began drawing tiny circles at the back of his neck, he thought he was going to lose all control. She tasted even better than he'd imagined.

The beat of the next song came over the sound system loud, and clear, and fast. Regretfully, he eased back and twirled her once again before tugging her away from the dance floor. At the bar, still holding on to her hand, not wanting to lose the connection, he ordered two glasses of water, handing her one and taking the other in his free hand. "I'd carry it back for you, but I selfishly don't want to let go of your hand." Had he actually said that out loud?

Her smile bloomed. "I like holding your hand." A deep rose singed her cheeks. "I like kissing you too."

Tugging her close enough to feel her breath fanning his neck, he barely kissed her lips before easing back. "We're going to have to find a way to do more of this."

"I like the sound of that."

Threading his fingers with hers, he smiled down at her. "How about a walk on deck?"

"If you don't let go of my hand."

"Not on your life." Forcing himself to let go of one hand, his grip remained firm on her other hand as he steered them out of the lounge. Halfway down the hall to the bank of elevators, his cell phone buzzed. "That's odd."

Looking down at his screen, he frowned.

"Something wrong?"

"It's my mother." Tapping his screen the call came on. "Hey, what's up?"

"Monica woke up. She can't find Bunny. She's totally beside herself. I've never seen her so inconsolable. Where did you put it?"

"Me? I didn't put it anywhere. She always carries it around as if it were more precious than gold." He looked to Ginnie. "Do you know where Monica put Bunny?"

Ginnie's gaze drifted skyward a second as she shook her head. "Last time I remember her having it was on the scavenger hunt, but now that I think about it, I don't remember her carrying it when we went back to the suite."

"Damn." He returned his attention to the phone. "Mom, we think she may have dropped it during the scavenger hunt. It was a bit chaotic with all the participants and the crazy photo shoots."

"I hate to ask this…"

"I know. We'll see what we can do."

"Bless you. Love you. And thank Ginnie for me."

Disconnecting the call, he slid the phone back into his pocket. "I'd gotten used to no one calling. I expected something unpleasant, but this might be worse."

"Let's start with Lost and Found."

"Good idea. And if that doesn't work, we'll backtrack our day."

"We'll find it." Ginnie squeezed his hand and he couldn't help himself.

Leaning over, he stole one quick kiss. "A guy could get used to this."

Her smile widened. "Let's go find Bunny."

CHAPTER FIFTEEN

Lost and Found was a bust. The ship had a collection of stuffed animals that could have been enough to open a shipboard toy store, but no Bunny. If not for the distraught child and knowing how much that rabbit meant to her, the evening would have been perfect.

"We'll start with the end of the hunt. That was the crew member from Costa Rica." Nick glanced away from the concierge desk and pointed down the hall. "We found him at the buffet hall. Let's try there first."

"Makes sense."

Still holding hands, Ginnie wracked her brains, trying to remember exactly when was the last time she'd seen Monica clutching her favorite stuffed toy. Coming out of the elevator banks, they cut across the ship's deck. The wind blowing softly, the moon shining brightly, it was the perfect scenario for a romantic walk under the stars, except they had a mission. An important mission.

Halfway across, she spotted the heartbroken fellow sitting on a lounger, staring out at the sea. Fresh air was always a good way to sober up. Ginnie slowed her steps. "Good evening."

At first the guy didn't seem to even hear her, then his gaze lifted and the pain in his eyes almost made her gasp. Had she ever seen so much sadness. "Evening." He cleared his throat. "You're the lady I bumped into earlier. Sorry about that."

"No problem." She smiled, thinking maybe she could lift his mood. "I've bumped into all sorts of things on this ship."

He nodded and shifted his gaze back to the ocean. The

conversation was over. Something tugged inside her, but she was no psychologist; whatever had this guy all broken up wasn't going to get fixed by her forcing a conversation. With a curt nod, she squeezed Nick's hand and kept walking.

"I know you want to help, but sometimes a man just needs to be alone."

"That's what my father says. Especially in the middle of a football game when Mama decides she wants to chat about Sunday's dinner menu."

Nick chuckled. "I seem to remember similar conversations with my mother and father, except Dad was trying to watch hockey and Mom would think that was a great time to discuss an upcoming vacation or someone's wedding."

"I guess marriage is pretty much the same all around." Though she couldn't say that about her sisters. Those two seemed to have a crazy connection with their spouses. Or maybe they were just still in the honeymoon phase of life—perhaps football and hockey games might become more critical down the road a few years, but somehow, she couldn't see it. Still, she wished being surrounded by so many happy couples she could have learned something brilliant to say and make that man feel better.

"He'll be fine."

She cocked her head at Nick. "How'd you know I was still thinking about the guy on deck?"

"You press your lips into a thin line when you're thinking, and I was pretty sure you aren't thinking about the weather."

"I didn't know I was that predictable."

He shrugged. "Not predictable at all. You are a woman, after all."

With a gentle smack of his arm, Ginnie chuckled. Nick did have a point—men were lousy at understanding women. Though, Nick seemed to be an exception. Much like her brothers-in-law. "Over there is where we caught sight of the staffer from Costa Rica. I do hope the bunny is around somewhere." Practically tugging him behind her, she hurried to the corner and letting go of Nick's hand, began searching under the tables, on the chair tops, in the corner. "Darn it. See anything?"

Several feet away from her, doing the same thing, Nick lifted his head. "Nothing."

They puttered around, expanding the search area slightly and then sighed.

Ginnie placed her hands on her hips. "Hey, on our way to this last stop, the kids were running around the lounge chairs."

"That's right." Nick snapped his fingers. "They were playing some kind of catch me if you can game. Maybe she dropped it then?"

Hurrying in that direction, Nick was only a few steps behind her. Reaching the first chair, she leaned over and tried to see underneath the lounger. The moonlight didn't provide enough illumination to see well. If she'd brought her phone she could have used the flashlight app, but the only people who would try to call was her mother and she wasn't in the mood for a day by day, blow-by-blow conversation of how the trip was going. Especially since right now she didn't quite know what she would say about her relationship with Nick. *Relationship.* Glancing down the row a short distance where Nick was moving and turning chairs trying to find his niece's favorite bunny, the sight brought a smile to her face. Before today, she would have said her crush on Nick was most likely one-sided. Now, she was pretty darn sure they had something, something she hoped wasn't going to end when they docked in home port or she'd be just as miserable as Mr. Heartbroken.

Circling back to what she was doing here, she moved on to the next seat. Nothing. Where the heck had Phoebe dropped the darn bunny? On a sigh, she stood upright and looked around. Her gaze fell on the railing across the deck. Blinking, she squeezed her eyes and focused. What? "Oh my God."

Nick's heart stuttered at the panicked sound of Ginnie's voice. The sight of her darting across the deck to the other side of the pool, practically vaulting over lounge chairs or anything else in her path, made the hairs on the back of his neck stand on end.

What the hell? Without hesitating a moment, he took off after her, finally seeing what she'd seen. Someone straddled the railing on the other side of the ship.

"Hello again," Ginnie's soft-spoken voice carried through the air as her steps slowed.

"Stay away!"

Nick recognized the voice. It was the man they'd seen just a short while ago on one of the lounge chairs. Mr. Heartbroken.

"Okay." Ginnie put both her hands up. "I'm not moving, but that's a pretty dangerous place to stargaze."

What the hell was she doing? Nick searched left and right, anywhere in hopes of seeing a crew member. Nothing. It was just the three of them out here. A ship as big as a small town and they were the only three out here. Insane.

"That's the whole idea," the man snapped.

"It really is a lovely evening," Her chin elevated, but her gaze fixed on the man, she barely inched closer.

Nick had to swallow the instinct to scream at Ginnie to stay back. Let the professionals handle this. Not that he didn't want her helping, but he was terrified if she got too close and the man really jumped, he might take Ginnie with him.

"The view is better from these chairs back here." She inched a little closer.

Staring down into the black ocean, the guy didn't seem to notice Ginnie was moving closer. "This was supposed to be the perfect honeymoon. Janice always wanted to take a cruise. Bask in the sun. Visit the beaches."

"Sounds lovely." Her gaze remained fixed on the man.

At the same slow pace Ginnie used, Nick inched his way closer to her.

"I have champagne in my cabin every night. And chocolate covered strawberries. Janice loves chocolate covered strawberries."

"I do too," Ginnie spoke ever so softly.

The man lifted his gaze and turned to her, then looked over her shoulder to Nick. "Don't get any closer."

Nick froze in place.

Ginnie held her hands up again. "If you don't want me to come closer, can you come back here so we can talk some more?"

"There's nothing more to say. Janice canceled the wedding with only forty-eight hours notice. Right about now she's in Vegas with Tommy Hamilton the third. His daddy owns the largest bank in Melville. The Cadillac dealership too. He was supposed to be my best man. Instead he got the best girl."

"I don't think so." Ginnie crept closer and Nick wanted desperately to reach out and snap her back closer to him, but he was still too far away to reach her. To protect her.

"Of course he did," the man snapped again, throwing his other leg over the railing so he was now sitting on the rail instead of straddling it.

Where the heck is the crew? Nick dared to drag his gaze away from Ginnie and look around again. Doesn't a ship like this have cameras everywhere? Nick pushed his sleeves up and dared to take another step; he had to get close enough to be able to grab her if he had to.

"No." Ginnie reached the railing. "The best girl would be here on her honeymoon. She doesn't deserve you."

"How would you know?"

She dared to rest her hands on the railing. "Because good women don't run off with another man two days before their wedding. If I were going to marry, I'd show up at the wedding."

The man shook his head and leaned forward.

"No." Ginnie shouted and climbed up onto the rail.

"Ginnie, no!" Nick moved closer still. Terrified if he rushed to grab her, the other guy would take the dive and it wouldn't take much for him to reach out now and make Nick's worst fear of taking Ginnie with him a reality.

Instead of answering, Ginnie held up her hand and

scooted to the left so she was almost an arms length from the potential jumper. "Do you know why I'm here?"

The man shifted his gaze to meet hers again. "What? No."

"My friend's six-year-old niece lost her stuffed bunny. She's heartbroken. My friend and I are here looking for the bunny. The last thing her father gave her. She misses her daddy."

For just a second his blank, emotionless expression softened. "I hope you find it for her."

"If you jump, someone's going to be heartbroken. Miss you the same as Monica is missing her daddy."

"There's no one."

"Your mother?" Ginnie inched a little closer.

That seemed to give him pause.

"If my mother is any example," Ginnie kept talking, "to them we're always their babies. She's going to feel guilty. Blame herself. Do you want her to blame herself because you jumped?"

His chest seemed to heave with a deep sigh. "It's not her fault."

"You know that, but will she? I doubt it. I already feel awful I didn't notice Monica lost her precious bunny. Your mother would be devastated if she didn't notice how sad you are."

"She still has my sister."

"But that's not her baby boy."

He seemed to lean back a bit. "How'd you know I was younger than my sister?"

"Doesn't matter. A mother always sees her grown son as her baby. My aunt Antonia drives my cousin Giovanni nuts when she tries to baby him."

"Mom is a nurturer."

For a fraction of a second, Nick thought he saw a hint of a smile on the man's face. Glancing about, there was still no one official anywhere in sight. He didn't even know how to call for help. Ginnie shimmied closer to the guy and Nick's stomach did a somersault. *Please Ginnie, don't.*

Her right arm waved for Nick to come around to her

right side. She didn't have to gesture twice. He eased to his right and as quickly as he dared, came up beside her.

"What do you say we go inside and you can tell me more about your mother?"

"Mom would like you. Tell her I love her and it's not her fault."

"You tell her!" Ginnie shouted, losing her calm for the first time.

"No." He stood up, only one hand tethering him to the ship. "There's no point."

In a flash, Ginnie flung herself left, her arms wide. Nick's arms wrapped around Ginnie's waist as her arms wrapped around the man's torso. In a huddled thud, all three landed back onto the deck. Nick had never been more thankful to God for his athlete's reflexes.

As he lay there on his back, his arms still tightly wrapped around Ginnie, he whispered, "Are you all right?"

"Ask an easier question," Ginnie muttered.

As the deck vibrated beneath him, the sound of thundering footsteps grew louder at the same time Mr. Heartbreak recovered from the surprise of the fall and began pulling away from them.

"Let me go!" he shouted. "I want to die. Let me jump!"

That's when Nick realized several crew had taken hold of him and an officer in white actually approached with a straight jacket. Who knew ships had straight jackets?

"May I help you up?" Another officer extended his hand to Ginnie.

Before she could move, Nick tightened his grip around her. "No, thank you. I've got this."

The officer looked down at him, frowning. "You sure?"

"I'm sure." Nick nodded and rolled around so he and Ginnie were on their side. "I just need to hold you for another minute. You scared the crap out of me."

"Sorry, but I had to do something." She snuggled into his shoulder. "You can hold me as long as you want."

"Good. I don't think I want to let go—ever."

CHAPTER SIXTEEN

Ginnie had been waiting for the chance to wear that little cocktail dress she'd packed for formal night. Since half the passengers were not on board for the original formal schedule, it had been postponed until all passengers were present. Now she wasn't so sure that wearing it was the right thing to do.

She still loved the dress, but somehow felt even more exposed than she had in the shop. Tonight was the first night everyone, including Theresa and Alan, were having dinner together and she didn't want to give the wrong impression. Channeling her inner little sister, she swallowed hard and closing her eyes, zipped up the dress before staring at herself in the mirror. It really did fit her like a glove. Shaking her head, she came within an inch of changing when a knock sounded on the door.

Without thinking it could be anyone besides the cabin steward, she flung the door open and came face to face with one Nick Maroney, more handsome than ever in his suit. "Wow."

Her hand flew to her cleavage. "I should change."

Shaking his head, Nick grabbed her hand. "Please don't. I want every man on this ship to be jealous that I'm with the prettiest girl onboard."

Knowing her cheeks were flushing at least a little pink, she spun around and grabbed her evening bag, before turning back. "I guess we're ready for dinner."

"Just a minute." Never moving his gaze away from her eyes, he tucked a loose strand of hair behind her ear, then leaned in for the sweetest quick peck on the lips. "Now we're ready."

Nick's family was already seated at the large table. Everyone dressed up and looking so elegant. Even the girls, including little Phoebe, had on pretty dresses and the boys button-down shirts. Settling in and placing orders, the conversation shifted to the other night.

"I would never have had the nerve to do what you did." Now that they were back onboard again, Nick's sister Theresa and her husband Alan were getting caught up on what the entire ship was still buzzing about.

"I didn't really do anything. At least nothing anyone else wouldn't have done." At the time all she could think of was not letting the man jump. She hadn't given any thought to how much danger she might be putting herself in.

Nick raised his hands. "I was there and my first thought was to find help, not wrestle the guy to the ground."

"Well," Ginnie shrugged, "that wasn't my thought either. I had honestly hoped with all the things I've talked my sisters and cousin out of through the years, that I'd do a better job of talking him into living."

"Don't sell yourself short," Mrs. Maroney chimed in. "When I went to the doctor for a follow-up on my foot, he told me that you couldn't have done a better job if you were a professional negotiator. Once they got him into sick bay, the doctor learned that you bringing up how his mother would be sad was how you were able to catch him off guard long enough to grab him. The doc decided to have him call his mother. After he spoke to her, he broke down crying. Once he gets off the ship, he'll be hospitalized for evaluation, but the doctor says that Bill is already doing better."

"Bill," Ginnie repeated. "Funny, I never even thought to ask his name."

"You might also like to know that there's a really nice nurse in sick bay who is helping cheer Bill up." Nick's mom smiled mischievously. "Ships really can be very romantic. I might have to bring your father on a cruise one of these days."

"You should," Ginnie agreed. "My mother keeps threatening to bring Dad on one to renew their vows."

"Oh, what a sweet idea." Theresa smiled.

Ginnie laughed. "Dad doesn't seem to think so. At least not yet, but I'm sure Mama will convince him sooner or later that a vow renewal on a ship is one of *his* better ideas."

All the adults at the dinner table chuckled. Nick's mom was getting around better with a little knee scooter they'd given her, the kids were doing another pizza movie night on deck, and Phoebe was at the toddler care. Everyone making the best of their last nights on board ship.

Ever since the excitement the other night, Ginnie had spent as much time as possible with Nick and his family. From the minute Theresa and her husband rejoined the cruise, Nick's sister had been full of stories about the misadventure. Once again the conversation had circled back to when the ship had to pull anchor.

"I honestly thought the island was going to blow away. The waves were so high."

"Theresa, they weren't that high."

She shrugged. "They were high enough. There were so many of us left ashore that the locals had to open their doors to us."

"Oh, that happened to my sister and her husband when they missed the sailing. Though in that case it was their fault," Ginnie said.

"We had a great time with a lovely couple. It was so much better than a hotel."

"That's a surprise." Mrs. Maroney tipped her head to one side. "I'd rather have room service."

"The house was huge and we stayed in the guest cottage. We had a great view of the ocean from our room every morning. The wife would bring us coffee and breakfast on the terrace. I'm telling you, no better way to spend a honeymoon."

"I'll keep that in mind," Nick teased his sister.

"Hey, Grandma." Jake came rushing up to the table.

"I thought you were at the movie?" his father asked.

"We are, but Monica is getting tired and was afraid she'd lose Bunny again so I told her I'd find you. Can you keep it safe for her?"

"Of course I can." Nick's mom beamed at her newest grandson. From what Ginnie had heard, the boys had been a little reluctant to call Theresa Mom, or Mrs. Maroney Grandma, but on this ship, they seemed to have turned a leaf and Mom and Grandma rolled easily off his and Jeff's tongue.

"We don't want to lose Bunny again," Theresa added.

"I still can't believe after everything, you guys still went hunting for Bunny." Mrs. Maroney shook her head. "I didn't know how we were going to get through the next twenty years without that rabbit."

"It wasn't that hard." Ginnie shrugged. "We walked past the soft ice cream shop and saw Bunny still sitting on the table top where Monica had left it."

"We'd actually forgotten that we stopped for ice cream after the hunt." Nick took hold of Ginnie's hand.

"The staff said they'd left it in plain sight in case anyone came looking for it, but made sure no one else took it." Ginnie would have preferred they'd just turned it into Lost and Found, but if they had, Bill might have successfully jumped.

"Okay if I go back to the movie now?" Jake asked his dad.

"Sure, kiddo." Alan nodded.

Jake turned on his heel and paused to face his uncle. "Thanks for finding Bunny, Uncle Nick. Monica is really happy now." Jake pivoted enough to face Ginnie. "Thank you too, Aunt Ginnie." And just like a shot, he was running around tables and out the door.

Staring in the direction Jake had run off, she realized her jaw was hanging slightly open and snapped it shut. Until now, the kids had been calling her Miss Ginnie. Where did aunt come from?

Squeezing her hand, Nick pushed to his feet and faced his family. "If you'll excuse us." He turned to Ginnie. "We need to talk."

Never in his life, had Nick been as nervous as he was right this minute. When the kids had asked him if he was going to marry Ginnie, he'd turned the question and asked them if they'd like to have Ginnie for an aunt. Apparently, Jake had just given their answer.

"I hope Jake didn't upset you by calling you Aunt Ginnie?"

Ginnie shook her head.

"Good." He led them up a flight of stairs and out on deck. "I'm going to miss this."

"The stars at sea are amazing." Ginnie stared up at the sky.

He tugged on her arm and curled her into his personal space, letting his hands fall gently on her hips. "I don't mean the sky or the sea or the stars."

Her cheeks tinted pink and he tugged her a little closer. "I've been talking with the front desk, and the manager, and even the captain."

"You talked to the captain? What about?"

"A lot happened on this cruise. It wasn't just the passengers like my sister and Alan and their families who were inconvenienced. Though to hear them tell it, this was the best thing to happen to them. We just won't share that tidbit with the cruise line."

Ginnie chuckled. "Probably not a good idea."

"Mom wouldn't have hurt her ankle if not for the rough seas, and I would have had to deal with the kids all on my own if not for you."

A soft gleam reached her eyes as her smile widened. "You would have managed."

"I would have survived, but no one would have had as much fun."

"It *was* fun. Thanks for letting me be a part of it all. Things might have been pretty boring for me without all of you."

"We can debate that another time." Swallowing hard, he pushed forward. "For now, what's important is that the cruise line agrees you were equally inconvenienced, and they appreciate the risks you took to prevent a man from going overboard. Though I suspect the bad publicity, they avoided didn't hurt any. They are giving you a free cruise, the same as they are for the families that were inconvenienced by pulling anchor."

"What?" Her mouth dropped open again and Nick had to resist kissing the surprise off her face.

"You're getting a free cruise out of this mess."

"Wow." She blinked and frowned. "A cabin all to myself?"

"Up to you."

Her expression remained serious. "Can I bring someone?"

"Again," he shrugged, "up to you."

A smile replaced the frown. "Gee, I wonder who I could invite?"

He pulled her in closer, placing a finger under her chin, lifted her face and stepped in for a kiss. Nothing hurried, not a quick *happy to see you* peck on the lips, but a slow, sensitive, gentle touch in an effort to convey everything he felt for Ginnie, and more.

When they came up for air, he blew out a slow sigh and rested his forehead against hers. "I understand cruises make excellent honeymoons."

Ginnie didn't say a word, she barely nodded.

Foreheads still touching, his eyes closed, he prayed he was doing this right and not about to scare off the only woman who ever made him feel this way. "Of course, I'd need a wife to take a honeymoon."

The moment the words were out of his mouth, Ginnie tipped her head back and stared up at him.

"I don't think I'm saying this right." Getting down on one knee, he looked up at her. "I should have a ring, and if you say yes, I'll buy you whatever you want. And if you need more time, I can wait. But Giovanna Ummarino, I cannot imagine going back to living a single day without you in it. Would you do me the honor and blessing of being my wife?"

The way she stared down at him so long, he thought she was searching for a polite way to say no. Finally, she kneeled down in front of him. "Am I dreaming?"

He shook his head.

"You really want to marry me?"

"Very much."

A slow smile pulled at her lips and she threw her arms around him, knocking them both onto the hard deck. "Yes, yes, and *hell yes*."

EPILOGUE

"This is so very exciting." Antoinette Ummarino stirred the homemade gravy one last time before scooping out the carrots. Like her mother and her mother before her, she'd used the carrots in the weekly gravy-making ritual to take the edge off the bitter tomatoes. Whenever she tasted gravy made with sugar, she'd grimace and frown and come just short of spitting it out.

"What is so exciting?" With a beer in his hand, Giovanni Ummarino straightened and closed the refrigerator door. "Family dinner?"

Rolling her eyes, his aunt sighed. "You know I love Sundays. The whole family here. Everyone laughing, playing, and eating."

Of course eating. They were Italians, the word was almost synonymous with eating. If he'd heard his aunt Antoinette say *mange* once, he'd heard it a thousand times from her and every mother, aunt, and grandparent in the clan.

"So what's so exciting?"

Flashing that coy smile that often came before some idea that hardly ever sat well with the receiver, she stared wistfully out the window. The wistfulness didn't offset the nerves turning in his gut at the smile that usually came right before she volunteered a family member to do something they didn't want to do. "I'm finally going to have grandchildren."

"Grandchildren?" He glanced out the window at the family enjoying the sunshine and warmth ushered in with the start of summer. "Who?"

"Anyone."

Had his favorite aunt finally lost her mind? Taking another look, he studied his cousins. Mina and Kent had been married a couple of years now, even though to his eye they still looked like newlyweds. Every time that man looked at Mina, any fool could see how much he loved her. Same thing for Mina when she was near Kent. Jo was the same story. She and Dylan had been married just over a year and like the eldest Ummarino daughter, was happy as the proverbial clam. Those two looked as nauseatingly cute as they did the day they came home from the cruise where they met. Neither of the women looked to show any signs of being pregnant.

Playing croquet, Ginnie and her fiancé were doing more flirting than playing. Watching them smile at each other, bump shoulders, blow kisses, or momentarily grab hands and squeeze, for Giovanni was somewhat entertaining and just a bit nauseating. He couldn't picture himself ever being so doting over a woman. At least Nick was a nice guy, and Giovanni, or Johnny as anyone outside the family called him, liked him just as much as his other cousins' husbands. They'd all found their soul mates, but he couldn't picture Ginnie pregnant before the big wedding cruise. Even if the two did look like they were glued together at the hip.

So what was his aunt talking about?

Still eyeing his cousins, he watched Ginnie and Nick, hand off their mallets, hold hands, and march toward the house.

Maybe his aunt was merely voicing wishful thinking?

"You look perplexed." Ginnie came in the back door, her fiancé at her side.

"Just thinking about something your mother said."

"Don't think too hard, your head may start to hurt." Ginnie pulled a cola out of the fridge and handed it to Nick.

The guy received the drink with a smile. With his free hand, he tugged his fiancée into his arms and giving her a not too quick peck on the lips, softly uttered, "thank you" in a tone so deep and sultry that any woman would probably fall into his arms now and ask questions later. Except there was only one woman, he had eyes for and she was already in his arms.

"None of that in my kitchen." Ginnie's mother smacked her girl on her behind and kept walking toward the pantry.

"Practicing, Mama, practicing," Ginnie teased back.

The back door squeaked open and Mina carried in an empty bowl of chips. "The masses are starving."

"Hold your horses." His aunt waved a wooden spoon at her eldest daughter. "Tell the masses the pasta is almost ready."

Another moment and Jo came into the kitchen as well. "Aunt Maria wants to know where her salad is."

"In the fridge. Your cousin Rosa tossed it a little while ago."

The sisters mulled around the kitchen, helping their mother feed an army. Not that he knew very much about pregnant women but he didn't see anything different about any of Aunt Antoinette's daughters.

"Hey, as long as you're all here." Giovanni crossed his arms. "Which one of you is pregnant?"

All three sputtered, stammered, dropped their jaws, and blinked back their bulging eyes.

"Giovanni Ummarino, what's the matter with you?" His aunt scowled at him. "When did you become a blabbermouth?"

"Since my curiosity got the better of me." He spun around to face his cousins again. "So, who is it?"

"Don't look at me." Ginnie shook her head and opened the fridge again, pulling out Aunt Maria's salad.

Jo and Mina looked at each other, then each gave a slow shake of the head.

"No one?"

All heads in the room turned from side to side.

"Aunt Antoinette, why are you messing with me? No one's pregnant."

His aunt shrugged her shoulders.

"Why would you tell cousin Johnny that one of us is pregnant?" Mina stared at her mother.

"You know how often your father gets a toothache?"

All the sisters rolled their eyes, but it was Mina who

spoke up. "Yes, Mama. Three times in his life."

"That's right." Mina's mom nodded. "When I was pregnant with each of you." The family matriarch waited a moment before continuing. "You know how I feel about olives."

"You don't like them," Jo answered quickly.

"Except?" their mother prodded.

This time it was Ginnie to answer. "When you were pregnant with the three of us."

"Exactly. And do you know what happened yesterday?"

Everyone in the kitchen shook their heads.

"I went grocery shopping for Sunday supper ingredients, and I bought olives."

"So you bought olives? So what?" Giovanni asked.

His aunt's head whipped around to face him. "And today, your uncle woke up with a toothache. I know I'm not the one who's pregnant so that means only one thing."

"That Uncle Vito needs to go see a dentist?"

"No." She waved a frustrated arm at her nephew. "At least one of my girls is going to have a baby."

"At least?" Mina and Jo echoed.

"Like I said," Ginnie flashed a toothy grin at her sisters, "not me."

Simultaneously the voices in the kitchen suddenly grew louder and faster and Giovanni had a feeling that his aunt might be right after all.

Coming up beside him, his aunt leaned in. "I didn't tell them, but I bought two jars of olives." And just like that, grinning, his aunt went back to her pot of gravy.

Two olive jars could only mean one thing, the next generation of Ummarinos might share a birthday, and he was definitely going to relish his role as Uncle Johnny.

Enjoy an excerpt from
Just One Date

"Our grandfather, a man richer than Bezos, offered to pay for the wedding, and the future Mrs. Andrew Mason told him no?" Chase James Baron, head of Baron Enterprises and confirmed bachelor, tipped his brandy snifter at his sister Eve. "The more I learn about Nancy, the more I like her."

As far as their grandfather, a former Marine turned politician, was currently concerned, each of his grandchildren should have six children—just as he and his wife of sixty years had done. Andrew's mother, Amanda Baron Mason, was the youngest and closest in age to Chase's father, Bradley Baron. Bradley had garnered his father's approval by marrying young, and well, although he only had five children, instead of the expected six. Unfortunately for Bradley, divorcing Chase's mother and working his way through three more wives had not gone over nearly as well with the proud former governor. Even if the unions had added two more grandchildren to the fold.

Now their grandfather was clearly tiring of waiting for his grandchildren to continue the tradition of having a large family. So far, much to former Governor James Earnest Baron's chagrin, every last one of his progeny was woefully behind the curve in finding a spouse and increasing the troops—his loving reference to his family. Except for Andrew, who had been caught and reeled in by his new bride-to-be.

Andrew and Nancy's nuptials had brought Chase to Galveston in preparation of the first, long-awaited, wedding of his generation. He and his siblings, Craig, Mitch and Eve were waiting for their brother Kyle onboard his yacht—a favorite family gathering spot—to leave for a quiet sail along the Gulf coast before the upcoming festivities, and ensuing chaos began.

"You're going to love Nancy," his sister Eve said with a smile. "Smart and sassy. Perfect for Andrew. Even though the Governor grumbles about her stubbornness—often—I think he really likes her."

"If it means finally having a great-grandchild, I think he'd let Lucrezia Borgia into the fold." Chase would have laughed at his own joke if he didn't think it held a grain of truth. "At least Andrew and Nancy will take the pressure off the rest of us grandchildren to breed."

Eve almost snorted her brandy. "What planet are you living on? If anything it's made the Governor more determined to increase the family troops. Oh, wait. That's right. You hide out in your Dallas man cave. Sleep, eat, and breathe Baron Enterprises. I must say, moving the operations to the downtown high rise, including a penthouse apartment, made for an affordable commute. You never even have to leave the building. Ever."

"Now you sound like the old man." Ten years ago when Chase had first come up with the mixed-use plans for the new headquarters, his grandfather had been delighted with the idea. Chase and his cousin Devlin, founder of one of the largest commercial real estate firms in the country, had worked out every detail before presenting it to their grandfather. That had been long before the patriarch had become obsessed with seeing his grandchildren procreate.

"Never gonna meet a good woman if you live behind that desk. Balance, boy. Balance," Chase mimicked his grandfather.

"You can take the man out of the military, but you can't take the military out of the man. Push, push, push." Eve tipped her head back and blew out a sigh. "Did you hear what he did to Craig?"

"At Mitch's fund-raiser last month?"

Eve nodded. "Craig made the mistake of telling the Governor that he was going stag to our dear brother the senator's event."

"Craig runs a major production company. Surely an up-and-coming actress would have been more than happy to have her photos splattered across every media outlet under the sun at a ten-thousand-dollar-a-plate dinner for the senate's golden boy."

"I don't think any of us realized the Governor has upped the ante. If we can't find our own dates, he'll find someone for us."

"And that is exactly why I am bringing my own date." Chase pushed to his feet and crossed the lounge of his brother's yacht to refill his drink. One of the stuffiest families on the social registry, the Van Kleins had married off all their children but one. And from his limited interactions with Gwyneth, her spinsterhood was for good reason. "I can't help but wonder, what was the Governor thinking, sticking Craig all night with Gwyneth Van Klein?"

Eve raised a single brow at her eldest brother, then shook her head. "The usual. Good stock. Wide hips. I swear, in this day and age, the old man still thinks of women as brood mares. He probably has Gwyneth's dental records."

"I'd be more worried that he probably has yours." Kyle, the missing sibling, came through the doorway. "Sorry I'm late. My meeting ran long. I see you've already helped yourself to refreshments."

"We skipped the lemonade and went straight for the hard stuff." Eve smiled up at him.

"My Napoleon brandy." Kyle laughed. "Rough week?"

"The Governor gave me a lecture on my biological clock yesterday. And the day before—"

"And this morning," Kyle added, his eyes filled with sympathy. "Sorry, sis."

"I'm used to it. It's not like I don't want to meet a nice guy, but it's not easy when your last name is Baron."

Unfortunately, Chase knew exactly what she meant. Having a family fortune prominently reported for all to see, the Baron name was a golden ticket for swindlers and fortune hunters. He'd been there, done that, even bought the wardrobe. Which is why he'd decided, before ever setting foot near Galveston for his cousin's wedding, to preempt the former Governor's unwanted efforts to find his offspring suitable mates. Chase might not run a major film production company, but he'd seen *Pretty Woman*. While he wasn't stupid enough to hire a hooker to appease his grandfather's matchmaking attempts, Chase wasn't beyond hiring a good actress to redirect their grandfather's attention elsewhere.

The plan had merit. Strictly business. No emotions. No gold diggers. And best of all, no complications.

"You're getting paid to spend the next seven days with a man?" C. J. Lawson's head was ready to explode from her sister's latest crazy plan.

"Yes and no." Bev shrugged.

C.J. glared at her younger sister the same way she'd stare down a raw recruit and then drew upon years of military discipline not to scream in Bev's face. "You do realize those answers do not go together."

"Yes, for five thousand dollars now and five thousand at the end of the week, I'm being paid to spend one week with Chase Baron but no not '*with*' with him."

"Do you know where you're staying?"

"Galveston."

C.J. refrained from rolling her eyes at her Pollyanna-like sister. "In a hotel?"

Nibbling on her lower lip, Bev hesitated a few minutes. "Maybe. He might have mentioned a boat."

"Okay." Who would have thought dealing with boots fresh off the bus would be easier than shaking some sense into her starry-eyed sister? "Maybe in a hotel, or a boat, but definitely in separate rooms?"

"Oh." Bev stopped tossing clothes into her suitcase. "I didn't ask."

Oh, brother. Never before had C.J. wished so hard that

Bev had gotten a few less beauty genes and just a teensy-weensy bit more of the brains in the family. At five foot five and 110 pounds, with a twenty-four inch waist, and blue eyes the shade of an azure crayon, Bev conjured images of Marilyn Monroe, Judy Holiday, and a long list of talented women who got more from sex appeal than smarts. "How could you not ask about sleeping arrangements?"

"Because, for ten thousand dollars, I don't really care if he puts me on the roof."

"Or in his bed?"

Sweater in hand, Bev froze and looked up at her sister. "That wasn't part of the negotiations."

All set to ask "What negotiations?" since her sister didn't seem to have any answers other than a 10K salary in a one-week time frame, and something about fooling an old man, C.J.'s mind suddenly registered that Bev held a sweater. "Why are you packing cold-weather clothes for Galveston?"

"Oh, well, that's what I was getting around to explaining."

That pixie twinkle in Bev's eye was never a good sign. As a kid it could have meant anything from teaching the unwilling cat how to swim, to homemade hair dye. Neither of which had produced stellar results. "Then explain. Again."

"Okay." Bev flipped her long blonde hair behind her shoulder and sucked in a deep breath. "Chase's cousin is getting married in eight days. It's a big family wedding. All the siblings and cousins and aunts and uncles will be there. Even his mom, who is practically a hermit somewhere in Europe, is crossing the pond for her favorite nephew's wedding."

C.J. bobbed her head, encouraging her sister to get to whatever part of this plan she hadn't already heard.

"So Chase has this grandfather."

"Yes," C.J. quipped a bit impatiently. "You've mentioned that before. He wants to see all his grandchildren married. I got that part."

"Well, the Governor—"

"Governor?"

"That's the grandfather. Former governor of Texas, though I think it was a lot of years ago, and before that he was a Marine."

"*Is*," C.J. said without thinking.

"Oh, yeah." Bev sighed and echoed with her sister, "*Once a Marine, always a Marine.*"

"Right." C.J. nodded again, sorry she'd derailed her sister's story.

"To avoid the grandfather harassing and annoying and prodding and matchmaking and creating family drama at his cousin's wedding, I've been hired to be his date. Like *Pretty Woman.*"

"You do remember she was a hooker?"

"Julia Roberts?"

Lord, C.J. loved her sister. Really she did. But the girl had tested C.J.'s patience from the day their parents had brought Bev home from the hospital. "Vivian—the character in the movie—Vivian was a hooker."

"Oh, yeah. Whatever. He offered me 10K to be his date." Bev stopped and, biting on her lower lip again, raised her gaze to the ceiling in thought. "Maybe it was *girlfriend.*" Smiling, she bobbed her head. "That was it. His girlfriend for a week."

"*Girlfriend.*" C.J. could hear the whine in her voice. She hated people who whined. "And you didn't ask about sleeping arrangements?" Why couldn't Bev be something normal, like a manicurist or receptionist? Why an actress? "Never mind. Can we get back to the clothes?"

"Oh. Right." Bev perked up. "This morning I got a call from my friend Gloria. You remember Gloria?"

C.J. nodded. She had no clue who the heck Gloria was, but C.J. had no intention of letting this conversation go down another rabbit hole.

"Gloria got a small part in John Cipro's new movie. It's a minor character, but they need a lot of extras because they're filming out in the middle of nowhere, and she got me on the list of extras! If they like me, I might even get to say something." Bev practically jumped in place with glee.

"At least that's a legitimate gig. When does filming start?"

"Monday."

"This Monday?" Now C.J. was really confused.

"Yes. In Canada, where it's cold."

At least that explained the sweater. "So, why are we having this conversation, if you're not taking the job in Galveston?"

"Because you are."

Read more of Just One Date available now, or at a discount directly from Chris.

MEET CHRIS

USA TODAY Bestselling Author of dozens of contemporary novels, including the award winning Aloha Series, Chris Keniston lives in suburban Dallas with her husband, two human children, and two canine children. Though she loves her puppies equally, she admits being especially attached to her German Shepherd rescue. After all, even dogs deserve a happily ever after.

More on Chris and all her books can be found at
www.chriskeniston.com

Follow Chris' Monday Blog at her website
ChrisKenistonAuthor

Follow Chris on Facebook at
ChrisKenistonAuthor

Never miss a New Release!
Sign up for News from Chris:
www.chriskeniston.com/newsletter.html

Questions? Comments?
I would love to hear from you! You can reach me at:
chris@chriskeniston.com

www.ingramcontent.com/pod-product-compliance
Lightning Source LLC
Chambersburg PA
CBHW061546310726

48972CB00008B/2638